D0615553

Mr. Robbins
Rides Again

Books by Edward Streeter

DERE MABLE

DAILY EXCEPT SUNDAY

FATHER OF THE BRIDE

SKOAL SCANDINAVIA

MR. HOBBS' VACATION

MERRY CHRISTMAS, MR. BAXTER

MR. ROBBINS RIDES AGAIN

MR. ROBBINS
RIDES
AGAIN

by

EDWARD STREETER

drawings by

MARC SIMONT

HARPER & BROTHERS, NEW YORK

To Judy (alias Dolly)

stubborn ingrate that she is

I love her still

r. Horace Robbins entered the front door of his Dutch Colonial house and tossed his hat on the telephone table. The cool, ordered front hall was like an oasis after the hot disorder of the commuting train.

"Hi," he called, to no one in particular.

Mrs. Robbins appeared at the entrance to the living room. "Hi, darling," she said. "I have some news for you. Guess who I had lunch with today."

"Who?" asked Mr. Robbins, who hated this peekaboo approach to a subject but found it less time-consuming to co-operate.

"Jane Weller."

"Jane who?"

"Oh, darling, don't be dense. You remember the George Wellers perfectly well. We met them in Florida last winter. Well, anyway, Jane asked me to have lunch with her and of all things they are going to the Bar Z Bar Ranch, too, and they want to drive out with us in our car. Of course I told her we'd be delighted."

"Why?" asked Mr. Robbins.

"Horace, don't be difficult. First of all, what else could I have said and anyway you told me when we came home from Florida that you liked the Wellers and hoped we'd see more of them. It's really awful that we haven't looked them up when they live so near to us. Why aren't you pleased to have company on the way out?"

"I am, I am," said Mr. Robbins, "but don't forget that we decided to go to a ranch this summer on account of that grandson of ours. I want this to be Bobby's vacation. I want to do things with him—ride and fish and explore places—"

"All right, darling, O.K. But can't the Wellers be there, too? You'd better pull yourself together; they are coming over this evening to talk about the trip."

Several hours later the Wellers arrived in gala mood. Mrs. Weller was a large, bony woman who obviously knew where to buy her clothes and whose fading blond hair had been faultlessly groomed in the latest mold— rather a dashing person on the whole who, had she been a man, might have made an excellent cavalry officer of the old Austrian school.

Her husband, on the other hand, was a delicate-featured man who only rose to her shoulder, a deficiency which he tried to overcome with a military-looking mustache and a habit of shouting at the slightest provocation.

Mrs. Weller entered the Robbinses' living room with her arms outstretched dramatically to no one in particular. "I can't believe it's true," she cried. "To think of the four of us being together for a whole month! I was so excited when I found that you were going to the Bar Z Bar too and Sally asked us to drive out with you that I dashed right down to the AAA and spent the whole afternoon having them map out the best route."

The shadow of a frown passed over Mr. Robbins' usually jolly face. He and Mrs. Robbins motored everywhere and if there was one thing he thought he could pride himself on, it was how to find his way around the United States. Quite obviously this was something that had best be made clear right at the start. "Sally and I have driven across the country so many times that we like to pick our own routes," he said. "This time we thought we'd go through Canada to Michigan and then swing west under Lake Superior. That's about the only way we haven't tried."

Mrs. Weller, in the act of spreading out a map on the living-room table, looked up in astonishment. "But Horace, what's the sense in going way up into the wilderness? You're not looking for the Northwest Passage or anything. Now, look. Here's how the AAA people have routed us and they certainly know the best way. We go on the Turnpike to Chicago—"

"I'd like to see Chicago again," said Mrs. Robbins, dreamily. "I haven't been there since I was a little girl. My Aunt Barbara—"

"We don't go through the city *itself*, dear. Heaven forbid. We cut around to the south of it and then, the first thing you know, we're out on the prairies."

"Yippee," cried Mr. Weller, helping himself to a Scotch and soda. Mr. Robbins did likewise and remained silent.

There was a pause which threatened to become embarrassing.

"Well, I suppose that's as good a way as any," said Mrs. Robbins, who was allergic to argument. "But there's one thing Horace and I feel very strongly about. This is going to be a leisurely trip. We want to get away from this constant hurry, hurry, hurry. I don't want to be hurried for a whole month."

"George and I feel just the same way," said Mrs. Weller, reassuringly. "We want to get out into the big country as quick as we can and then simplify our lives."

"And one way to do that is not to take too much luggage," said Mr. Weller, glaring meaningfully at Mr. Robbins. "Travel light. That's my motto."

"Righto," replied Mr. Robbins, still irritated. "Just

a spare breechclout and a pouch of dried corn. My motto is, 'Nothing carried, nothing lost.'"

Mr. Weller looked at him suspiciously and changed the subject. "What cameras are you taking?" he asked. "We ought to co-ordinate our cameras."

"I only have one," said Mr. Robbins.

"What kind is it?"

"Gracious, I don't know. Sally gave it to me for Christmas. It takes pictures about this size."

"Well it doesn't really matter too much. I'll take my Gramoflex 300 and my motion-picture outfit. I guess I'd better take along my telephoto lenses. We'll probably get some game shots."

"On the pack trip," said Mrs. Weller.

"We hadn't planned on a pack trip," said Mrs. Robbins. "Horace hates them."

"Oh, darling, everyone takes a pack trip. You can't say you've been West unless you've wandered around after a string of mules for a few days."

"Jane can bring her stereo," said Mr. Weller. "As a matter of fact, Horace, you won't need to bring your camera at all. That will cut one item at least."

"You don't mind if we bring our grandson, do you?" asked Mr. Robbins.

"Not at all," said Mr. Weller.

Mr. and Mrs. Robbins had planned to start their trip on Saturday but Mrs. Weller had pointed out that Saturday was a bad day to start anywhere if you lived around New York. As a result Mr. Robbins had rearranged things at his office so that the take-off could be made on Friday.

He had once read a book by Anne Morrow Lindbergh called *North to the Orient.* In it she had described how, in preparation for their flight to Japan, she and her husband had laid out their gear on the spare-room floor and then spent weeks eliminating unessential items.

Irked by Mr. Weller's admonition to travel light, Mr. Robbins had done likewise. He spent whole evenings eliminating articles and then putting them back again on the beds. Bit by bit, however, favorite sport shirts, slacks and the cherished trivia of vacation days were returned to the bureau drawers and camphor-scented cartons from which they had come. At last the residue, neatly baled into three suitcases and a small duffel bag, stood ready in the front hall.

On the evening before D-day Mr. Robbins drove

over to the Wellers' to pick up the latter's luggage so that he could pack the car that night.

"Come in," said Mr. Weller, "if you can find a place to stand." The front hall was blocked with baggage. "It's a bit more than we anticipated, old man, but you've got a station wagon so there'll be plenty of room."

"You ought to see what I made him leave behind," called Mrs. Weller gaily from the floor above. "Now, George, remember that heart of yours and don't try to carry those big bags. Horace and I can manage them perfectly. I'll be right down, Horace dear."

"Don't bother," said Mr. Robbins. "I can handle them all right."

As he staggered down the front steps with the last

load his breath was coming in quick sobs and his clothes were soaked.

"You're a sweet," called Mrs. Weller from an up-stairs window. "I do hope that wasn't too much for you. I'd have helped but I just got out of a bath as you drove up. You wouldn't want a wet nude running in and out, I'm sure. My, we're going to have a lot of fun. I can't wait."

"Good-by, old man," said Mr. Weller from the doorway. "See you at eight. Get a good sleep."

Mr. Robbins waved feebly in the direction of the house as he turned the switch key. It occurred to him that he could not recall having heard that there was anything wrong with George Weller's heart.

A few minutes after eight the following morning Mr. Robbins, who had been up since five, wiped his forehead with a grimy forearm and reviewed his labors. The rear of the station wagon was packed from floor to roof so solidly that it gave the appearance of masonry. Spread on the driveway behind the car was a litter of small objects for which there was obviously no room. Mr. Robbins stared at them unseeingly. The Wellers swung briskly around the corner of the house looking like models for a sport-clothes ad.

"All aboard that's going aboard," called Mr. Weller, cheerily.

"I've got to take a bath," said Mr. Robbins.

"Nonsense," snorted Mrs. Weller. "Tomorrow night's Saturday. We're almost ten minutes behind schedule now." She glanced at the bulging car. "Good gracious, Horace, we're going to need a periscope to drive. You and Sally must be taking everything but your horses. Where *are* Sally and Bobby? We really ought to get going."

Mrs. Robbins and Bobby appeared at the back door. Bobby was dressed in the local department store's version of a cowboy outfit, complete with two guns. The

latter were loaded with caps and he emerged from the
house in a rattle of gunfire.

"Gracious," said Mrs. Weller, "do we have to have
that all the way out?"

"Never point a gun, Bobby," said Mrs. Robbins.

"Wyoming, here we come!" shouted Mr. Weller,
climbing into the front seat.

"What in the world are you going to do with all
those odds and ends, Horace?" said Mrs. Robbins, glancing at the litter surrounding her husband. "We certainly
don't want them around our feet. I don't know why it
is that Horace always insists on bringing so much old
junk."

They glided westward on the Pennsylvania Turnpike, the wind roaring jovially through the open windows, the speedometer reading seventy and steady.

"Now," said Mrs. Weller, in the tone of one who lays down one task and picks up another, "let's organize a little. George will be treasurer. He's awfully good at that sort of thing. Each family will chip in fifty dollars and every time George shoots the hundred we'll pass the hat again."

Mr. Robbins winced. He had planned carefully for this trip. He wished that Mrs. Weller wouldn't treat it like an open crap game. "Why don't I give him everything I have?" he asked. "Then when he shoots that he can include me and save his ammunition."

"Nonsense, Horace. You've got a satchelful and you know it. Then I think we should adopt one basic road rule. Start early and stop early!"

Bobby pricked up his ears. "Are we nearly there?"

"No, dear. We won't be there for days and days and days." The enormity of this statement left Bobby speechless. He emptied several inches of caps through the open window to relieve his feelings.

"I certainly vote for stopping early," said Mr. Robbins. "Joe Hallowell told me of a swell place to spend the night outside of Cleveland. That's an easy run with a turnpike all the way."

"I forgot to tell you," said Mrs. Weller, "I've already reserved rooms in a motel near Toledo."

"Did you order dinner?" asked Mr. Robbins, but his words were torn away by the wind.

"**I**'m getting sleepy," said Mr. Robbins.

"Good gracious, dear, you never go to sleep at this time of the morning."

"So what?" said Mrs. Weller. "If he's sleepy, he's sleepy. No use landing in a ditch just because this is a wacky time to fold up. We might as well start rotating. George drives next. I go up front. You move over, Sally, and let Horace take your place. If we don't do things in an orderly way nobody'll know where they're supposed to go next." She looked over the top of the seat at Bobby. He was sound asleep. "For heaven's sake what do you people do at *night?*"

Mr. Robbins pulled the car over onto the shoulder, crawled into the rear seat and was out in an instant, his head resting against the baggage, his mouth open.

"George," said Mrs. Robbins from the rear seat, "would you mind closing your big window and opening your little ventilator window? I'm getting blown to pieces back here."

"O.K.," said Mr. Weller, rolling up the window, "but I'm not going to open that little gadget. It roars so it drives me nuts."

"Well, we must have *some* air," said Mrs. Weller,

who had immediately closed both of her windows when she moved to the front seat. "How about opening that back window next to you, Sally?"

"It does something to my ears. Can't you open one of yours, darling?"

Without replying Mrs. Weller turned and touched Mr. Robbins lightly on the knee. "Horace," she said gently.

Mr. Robbins stirred uneasily, his head tipped far back like a man in a barber's chair. "Horace," murmured Mrs. Weller, as a hypnotist to his subject. "Put the window down beside you."

Mr. Robbins' hand automatically groped for the handle and lowered the window. His hat blew back among the suitcases and his bare head continued to roll to and fro along the top of the seat.

"When do we eat?" asked Bobby.

"Darling, it's only eleven o'clock. We're going to have a nice picnic lunch at half past twelve."

"I'm hungry. I wanna eat now."

"Well, I'm afraid you'll have to wait, dear."

"Why? My mother always lets me eat when I'm hungry."

"I'm sorry, Bobby. Just wait till lunch time."

Bobby allowed his body to fall limply against Mr. Weller and emitted a series of heart-rending moans.

"For heaven's sake give him something to eat," said Mr. Weller. "How can I drive while he's flopping all over me like a dying seal?"

Mrs. Robbins sighed. "The picnic basket's in front, Jane, right at your feet. I guess it's all right to give him a sandwich or something."

Bobby ate three ham sandwiches, four chocolate brownies and several bananas while Mrs. Weller gazed, unheeding, at the Pennsylvania countryside. Then he leaned back contentedly and went to sleep. A discreet silence fell over the group.

An hour passed. Mrs. Robbins leaned forward and gazed fondly at her grandson over the top of the seat. "He's so good," she murmured.

Bobby opened his eyes. "I'm going to be sick," he said.

"For heaven's sake, stop," cried Mrs. Weller. As her husband brought the car to a screeching halt they both leaped out, leaving the Robbinses to cope with their own.

Later they ate at a roadside table while Bobby again slept peacefully on the back seat. During most of the afternoon he continued to sleep with his head on his grandmother's lap. As the sun began to sink behind a mass of angry purple clouds he suddenly sat up. "I'm hungry," he said.

"Good heavens," said Mr. Weller. "The child's positively rhythmic."

It was late when they reached their motel. The bank of purple clouds had fulfilled their promise and for the last hour had been emptying themselves without restraint over Ohio's fertile farmlands. Yellow patches of light from the windows of the motel lit up the streaming cars lined up in front of the bedrooms.

The affable proprietor of the motel recognized Mrs. Weller as the group leader at first glance. He handed her three keys with an understanding smile, then glancing appraisingly at the rest of the party handed Mr. Weller two pitchers full of ice cubes.

The overhang of the roof formed a narrow gallery in front of the lighted windows. From its edge flowed a curtain of water. As they walked to their rooms they appeared to be moving behind a waterfall.

"Isn't this cozy," said Mrs. Robbins.

"You'll get everything soaked if you unload the car out in the rain," said Mrs. Weller. "Turn it around and back it under the roof. George and I just have two little overnight bags. He'll show you which they are. I'm going to put a couple of those ice cubes to work."

Mr. Robbins turned the station wagon around and backed its rear end under the gallery only to find that it was so close to the wall of the motel that he couldn't let down the tailboard. The sound of ice cubes being dropped into tumblers and the light laughter of the Wellers floated through the open window.

He moved the car forward. The rain was coming down like a shower bath. This time he could lower the tailboard, but there was no room for him to stand behind it. Back to the wheel again. The water was running down his neck now and his trousers were beginning to settle in folds over his shoes like those of Civil War statesmen.

Having worked the car into the right position he found himself faced with a new problem. The curtain of water from the roof no longer beat on the top of the car, but came down about six inches behind it, thundering on the lowered tailboard and splashing in Mr. Robbins' already dripping face.

Mr. Weller's head appeared in the window. He had a glass in his hand which he rested on the sill. "Sorry to leave all the dirty work to you, old man," he said, "but you packed the car so you're the only one who knows where things are. Jane and I have two little black bags. That's all we want."

"I can't see through this waterfall," said Mr. Robbins.

"Just a second." Mr. Weller reappeared in the window and directed the rays of a flashlight on the back of the car.

"I don't see ours," he said, moving the light over the pile of suitcases. "Why did you put all the big ones, that we're not using, in the back?"

"Why did your grandmother suck eggs?" muttered Mr. Robbins.

"I can't hear you, old man, with all this sloshing. We really don't want those big ones in our room to-night, but I guess there's nothing for it but to drag them all out. We can pack more intelligently in the morning." Mr. Weller sipped his drink philosophically.

Mr. Robbins leaned forward to seize the handle of a suitcase. The curtain of water struck him across his neck and shoulders, making a drumming sound on the tweed of his sport jacket.

"I think it's letting up a bit," said Mr. Weller.

Mr. Robbins succeeded in extracting one of Mr. Weller's big suitcases, which he set down carefully in the largest puddle available. He dove under the falls for another.

"Hey," cried Mr. Weller. "You're getting our bags wet." A moment later he appeared on the gallery with Mrs. Weller, who helped him drag their dripping suitcases to their room.

Mrs. Robbins' head appeared in the window. Mr. Robbins was beginning to feel as if he were watching a Punch and Judy show.

"Horace, why in heaven's name do you want to unpack the whole car when all we need is that little brown duffel bag?"

"It's a hobby with me," said Mr. Robbins.

They were rolling across the gently undulating farm-lands of northern Indiana on parallel bands of concrete which had begun at the western end of the Holland Tunnel and gave every indication of going on, hypnot-ically, forever. Suddenly a grimy smudge appeared on the western horizon. "Chicago!" shouted Mr. Weller, who could work up an ecstasy on a shoestring.

"Well," said Mrs. Weller, opening the map compart-ment, "it's about time for a route conference."

"Joe Hallowell takes this route all the time," said Mr. Robbins. "He told me just before we left that there was a new road that goes right *through* Chicago along the lake shore. 'Route 41,' he said. It runs all the way from the end of the toll road to Milwaukee. You go shooting right through."

"I wouldn't dream of it," said Mrs. Weller, decisively. "I've got the whole thing marked on the map. We're going to cut around south of the city and they tell me you wouldn't know that you were within a hundred miles of it."

"How wonderful!" said Mrs. Robbins.

The toll road ended suddenly in a forest of belching chimneys. They turned south on a badly paved street lined with garages, filling stations, saloons and grimy factories. Two hours later they were still wedged in a stream of gigantic trailer trucks which moved glacierlike around the southern end of the city and then turned north. A burning slag pile emitted sulphurous yellow fumes which rolled across the highway.

"It certainly pays to avoid the big cities," said Mr. Robbins.

"Oh, come now. This doesn't last *long*," said Mrs. Weller. "You must expect a *few* signs of life near a city like Chicago."

"I'm going to be sick," said Bobby, tonelessly.

"Me, too," said Mr. Robbins.

They were free of Chicago at last. Mr. Weller picked up the *AAA Accommodations Guide*. "For goodness' sake let's get in on time *tonight*," he said. "I'm tired. Last night it was after seven." He glared at Mr. Robbins reproachfully.

"O.K., let's pick out our motel right now," said Mrs. Weller, taking the book from her husband's listless hands. "And then, Horace dear, you can phone ahead and reserve the rooms. Let's see. It's half past three now. Ha' past four, ha' past five, ha' past six—three hours, fifty miles an hour. That's a hundred and fifty miles. Now what good place is a hundred and fifty miles from here?" She consulted the map. "Here's a town called Buffalo Wallow. That's about a hundred and fifty miles from the dump we just went through."

"It sounds fascinating," said Mrs. Robbins. "Lots of old Western color. See if there are any nice motels there."

"Buffalo Wallow isn't mentioned," said Mrs. Weller. "The only places on this route that are listed are Madison and La Crosse. Madison's only seventy-five miles."

"We'd be there by five o'clock," said Mr. Weller.

"We certainly don't want to stop at five o'clock," said Mr. Robbins. "That's for sure. How far is La Crosse from Madison?"

"About a hundred and thirty miles. It's right on the Mississippi."

"Oh, let's go there," said Mrs. Robbins. "I can't imagine anything more fun than to lie in bed and hear the water gurgling against the levees, and to wake up—"

"There's a roadside phone," cried Mrs. Weller. "Here, you take the AAA book, Horace, and phone. We'll be across the street having an ice cream cone."

They were seated on the steps of the store, finishing their cones, when Mr. Robbins emerged dripping from the sun-baked telephone booth. "They'll hold them,"

he said. "But we'll have to get to work if we want to eat before every place closes."

"Good," said Mrs. Weller. "Well, it's your turn to drive, Horace, so you go right to work. That afternoon sun's going to be right in your eyes all the way. That's a shame."

"Drive carefully," said Mr. Weller. "I may take a snooze."

They sped through the rolling farmlands of southern Wisconsin, lush and green from the recent rains. The countryside was flooded with the amber light of late afternoon, which gave the great red barns an orange tint and deepened the shadows on the eastern slopes. "It's so beautiful," murmured Mrs. Robbins.

But Mr. Robbins saw none of it. There was only one thought in his mind—to reach La Crosse by seven-thirty. That was his goal. Like a road racer he half crouched over the wheel, his field of vision narrowed to the road ahead, which forever rushed toward him and endlessly disappeared under the front of the car.

With the sublime faith of those accustomed to being hurtled through a high-powered world his companions

chatted of this and that or dozed or looked about them with relaxed eyes. Mr. Robbins was unconscious of them. He had blended with the machine which he was guiding until man and motor were merged into a complex unity, focused fiercely and tensely on the task of unwinding the vast, undulating ribbon of the road— and staying on it.

It was after seven-thirty when they reached the Mississippi south of La Crosse. As they drew up in front of the motel Mr. Robbins slumped over the wheel like an exhausted oarsman. "What, here already," said Mr. Weller, waking up. "Why that didn't seem far at all."

"And such a beautiful drive," said Mrs. Robbins.

"I've always said," remarked Mrs. Weller, "that to really see the country you have to travel by car."

It was a beautiful cool morning and for once they were all up early. "We ought to *really* make time today," said Mr. Weller, rubbing his hands in anticipation of a record dash.

Mr. Robbins tried to unlock the back of the station wagon. The cylinder of the lock came out with his key, leaving the tail gate tightly bolted.

"It doesn't surprise *me*," said Mr. Weller. "I tell you, Horace, this car is a junk pile. Can't see why you ever bought one of them. You ought to have the whole thing looked over. Can't tell what's coming off next—"

"Mercy," said Mrs. Robbins. "In a big place like this there must be a service station that knows about these things."

The manager of the motel directed them to a great, immaculate shop run with clocklike precision by a young man with steely blue eyes and wavy hair. In his spotless white coat he looked more like a Hollywood surgeon than a super-garage mechanic. Yes, indeed. The back lock would be fixed in jig time. "Just pull the car over there, please," he said, whereupon he disappeared briskly and permanently.

The air hummed with efficiency. Purposeful mechanics hurried to and fro carrying their tool kits, or lay beneath cars gazing thoughtfully at their mud-caked bottoms. All this activity swirled around Mr. Robbins and his party as if they were the negative core of a magnet. The hands of the clock on the opposite wall moved slowly round the dial.

"Do you want me to go back and hold our rooms at that motel for another night?" asked Mr. Weller, sarcastically.

"What do you expect *me* to do?" asked Mr. Robbins. "Why don't *you* find somebody? I don't even *see* that chorus boy that runs the place."

An elderly man in a straw hat like those traditionally worn by stage farmers approached and inspected Mr. Robbins' license plate carefully. "New York?" he asked.

"Yes," said Mr. Robbins, shortly, his eyes continuing their search for the service manager.

"That a nice state," said the man, peering into all the windows as if he expected to see a corpse. "Where you heading?"

"Out West," said Mr. Robbins.

"Oh?" said the man, his tone indicating that this was an unusual situation. "My wife and I was in New York last summer. We got a daughter lives in Malone. Know that country?"

"Yes," said Mr. Robbins.

"Beautiful," said the man in the straw hat. "Ever take the ferry across Lake Champlain?"

"No," said Mr. Robbins. He had spotted the service manager on the other side of the room and started toward him. The man in the straw hat came along.

"Well," he said, "you've got a treat in store. Yes, sir, you certainly must do that. I'm surprised you haven't heard of it. My wife and I did it last year. We'd come East to visit our daughter. She married a boy from Malone."

The service manager was holding a consultation under the upraised hood of a car with two white-coated interns. Mr. Robbins circled the group, trying to catch someone's eye.

"My son-in-law's doing very good there," said the man with the straw hat, circling with him. "Hardware. Three fine children. But that ferry trip is certainly beautiful. My wife and I think there's nothing like it in the East."

"Excuse me," said Mr. Robbins, addressing the service manager, who immediately moved with his consultants to the other side of the engine.

"I've got a son living in Albuquerque," said the man in the straw hat. "Have you ever been to the Carlsbad Caverns?"

"No," said Mr. Robbins, plucking at the service manager's immaculate white sleeve. The latter turned to him with professionally controlled politeness.

"Yes, sir. What can I do for you?"

"Well, you've got a treat in store for you," said the man with the straw hat. "Those Carlsbad Caverns are the darnedest things you ever seen. There's one place—"

"You were going to have somebody take care of my car. The lock's broken."

The service manager swept the room with a harassed expression. "George," he said to a passing mechanic, "will you see what this gentleman wants?"

"I have another son lives in Little Rock," said the man with the straw hat, falling in between George and Mr. Robbins.

"What seems to be the trouble?" asked George.

Mr. Robbins handed him the lock with the key still embedded in it. "He's got five children," said the man with the straw hat. "The doctor says his wife can't have any more. She's got something the matter with her spleen."

"The back of the car's still locked," said Mr. Robbins. His group was waiting impatiently beside the car.

"It looks as if we'll have our picnic lunch in the garage," said Mrs. Weller.

"Have any of you ever been to the Carlsbad Caverns?" asked the man in the straw hat.

The service manager hurried up and had a consultation with the mechanic.

"It would almost pay you to come home that way if you ain't seen them," said the man in the straw hat. "I got a son in Albuquerque—"

"Why don't you all have lunch and come back about twelve?" said the service manager, soothingly. "We'll have everything ready for you."

"Gracious," said Mrs. Weller. "Do we have to eat lunch in the middle of the morning just because the lock's no good?"

"You'll enjoy that ferry trip," said the man in the straw hat.

"Try the Capital Café," said the service manager.

"I know," said Mr. Robbins. "That's where we've been eating since we left New York."

"It does seem," said Mrs. Robbins, "as if these things should have been looked over before we left home."

"You can't make a silk purse out of a junk pile," said Mr. Weller. "Well, let's eat."

South Dakota. The world had suddenly become enormous. In New York and New England no one noticed the sky. Here it was the dominant feature of the landscape, a great blue dome beneath which lazy, fat clouds moved unhurried. In the East the sky was the ceiling of the earth. Here, the earth was the floor of the sky.

It was a disk-like world in which the station wagon always stood in the exact center—a flat world carpeted with yellow clover blossoms and tufted, like a bedspread, with tree clumps each sheltering a big red barn and a small white house.

Ahead, the road bisected the disk, rising and falling but always pushing undeviatingly westward, its endless border of telephone poles looking fringelike in the distance. Mica, embedded in its surface, shimmered like water at the top of each rise. On the horizon the silhouette of a grain elevator pricked the skyline like a medieval watchtower.

"Uncle George, tell me about the time you were in the cavalry," said Bobby, bored by such large vistas.

"Oh, that's an old story, Bobby, and a long, long time ago," said Mr. Weller modestly.

"I know, but tell it again."

"Well, it was back in 1916," said Mr. Weller. "We were down on the Mexican border. In those days that was a dry desert country with nothing but mesquite and cactus—"

"Never mind all that stuff. Tell about how you used to charge."

"Well, Bobby, the cavalry troop would form a long line. The captain would be out in front. He would start the horses off at a walk, then we would draw sabres and trot. Then we'd break into a canter. Finally the captain would give the order, 'Charge,' and the whole outfit would gallop as fast as the horses could run, yelling like Sam Hill—"

"Yell," ordered Bobby.

Mr. Weller gave a piercing scream. Mr. Robbins, who was driving, swerved slightly and shuddered.

Bobby sighed. "Gee, I bet you ride better'n the Lone Ranger."

"No, no," said Mr. Weller, "just ordinary. Just so-so."

They rushed westward, the hot wind beating against the ventilator windows. The tree-sheltered farm buildings became further and further apart as the plowed fields gave way to grazing land.

"Where in the world are we going to eat our picnic lunch today?" asked Mrs. Robbins. "The only bits of shade in this country are full of ranch houses."

"Oh, we'll find something," assured Mrs. Weller. "It's only twelve."

"There's a tree," cried Mr. Robbins, pointing to a lone specimen about a mile down the road. It stood on the edge of a gully at the bottom of which a group of white-faced steers were swishing their tails thoughtfully. "We could climb under the barbed-wire fence. It's the only unattached tree in the state."

"I'd just as soon eat in a barnyard," said Mrs. Weller, scornfully. "Keep on. We'll find something better than that." Mr. Robbins wondered why it was that Mrs. Weller was never optimistic about anything but picnic sites.

They stopped for gas. "Are there any nice trees around here," asked Mrs. Weller, "where we could eat a picnic lunch?"

The man removed his cap and scratched his head. "Yes," he said finally. "Yes, there is. You go down the road about twenty-five miles an' you come to a town called Lummox. They's a mighty nice park there with tables 'n' everything." They thanked him and continued westward.

"Why couldn't we have eaten there?" asked Bobby.

"At a gas station? You don't want to eat at a gas station, do you, dear?"

"Why not? The man was eating *his* lunch there when we drove up. He doesn't have to go twenty-five miles to eat his lunch."

"Give him something out of the basket," said Mr. Weller quickly. "I can't stand that tune in my ear for the next half hour if I'm going to drive."

Lummox was a one-street town with a dusty park opposite the schoolhouse. There were tables and benches under the trees as the gas-station man had said. A hot wind had wrapped their legs in loose newspapers.

"No, no," cried Mrs. Weller dramatically. "Not here. I'd rather go back to the gas station. Keep on. Keep on."

West of Lummox all signs of human habitation ceased. The gray-brown, treeless prairies rolled away into emptiness on all sides. The sun beat down fiercely.

"Why don't we pull off on the side of the road and eat in the car?" suggested Mrs. Robbins.

"In this heat?" said Mrs. Weller. "Not me. Keep on."

They drove in strained silence for another ten miles. "There's a sign pointing to something," cried Mrs. Weller. "Slow down, won't you, so I can read it. There we are. 'Elks' Memorial Picnic Grounds.' You certainly can't beat that."

Below the level of the built-up highway was a small grove of trees, twisted and gnarled by the blasts of winter. Any vestiges of grass which might once have grown between their roots had long since been trampled into the dust. A crumbling outdoor fireplace had been used as a trash can until it overflowed, after which the Elks' guests had merely thrown their refuse over their shoulders. A table with a sticky top and two benches completed the décor.

"There," said Mrs. Weller, placing the picnic basket on the table in the midst of a swarm of protesting flies. "Could anything be cozier?"

Over the vast Dakota prairies the station wagon moved slowly. Actually it was rushing along at seventy-five miles an hour, but in those enormous spaces it was like a black ant moving across a tennis court.

Although the sun shone brilliantly on the road ahead there were storms all around them: isolated cloud masses of angry purple, spilling their watery contents onto the thirsty land in slanting gray curtains of rain. Flashes of lightning played through them and the air was filled with the sullen muttering of thunder.

It was a grand and sublime show—a super-spectacular —but the audience was unresponsive for the good reason that all but Mr. Robbins were asleep.

He himself felt drowsy, but there was no compromising with sleep for him. He was alone on the great prairies; as alone as Lindbergh had been as he fought sleep over the tossing waves of the Atlantic, as alone as Admiral Byrd buried beneath the snow in his Antarctic hut, as alone as the boy on the burning deck.

Those men could not falter, nor could he. Robbins sees it through. He swung around a right-hand curve. As Mr. Weller started to topple in his direction he reached out and gently pushed him back into an upright position.

The next morning the purple-gray sagebrush began to dot the brown earth, announcing the fact that they were in the West at last. Although there was still more than five hundred miles to go they felt that to all intents and purposes they had arrived.

It was afternoon before the Rockies came into view. They appeared suddenly behind a string of empty freight cars, their snow-covered tops sparkling in the brilliant sunlight, their blue-gray bases matching the sky above them so that the peaks seemed to be suspended in mid-air like a mirage—mirage mountains, siren mountains, forever luring those who struggled across these shimmering plains, be they lone mountain men or dust-covered wagon trains or vacationers in a station wagon.

It was long after dark, however, before they reached the foothills of the great rock masses which they had been watching for so many hours. A full moon rose above the black, saw-toothed edge of the mountains, lighting the road and glinting on the white water of the stream which rushed, headlong, beside it.

They saw a lantern hanging on a sign. By its dim light they read the lettering "Bar Z Bar Ranch" with an arrow painted underneath pointing into the darkness to their right.

They had arrived! The long trek was over. Its end was so simple, so sudden that there was something incredible about it. One minute you were rolling out of your driveway in Fairview Manor and the next you were surrounded by the Rocky Mountains. Mr. Weller leaned far out the open window. "Yippee," he yelled. His voice sounded small in the darkness.

As if in response, two figures emerged from the shadows. They were Tom and Mary Reims, owners of the Bar Z Bar, come to guide them up the canyon to the ranch.

The occupants of the car greeted them with the usual hysteria of travelers who have arrived unscathed at the end of a long journey. The initial outburst having exhausted itself, they followed the Reimses' jeep through a cattle gate and up a rough dirt road. Then they passed a number of log buildings and eventually the jeep stopped before a cabin among the pines.

"Here's your wickiup," said Tom Reims. He was a huge man who seemed to tower above them in the darkness. "It's really two cabins pushed together. You each have your own front door. We'll just help you unload your stuff and then we'll let you get some sleep. You must be pooped. You can unpack tomorrow."

"It's terrific," said Mr. Weller, gathering his strength for a final ecstasy. "I never smell hemlock without thinking of the trips I used to take into northern Canada. The woods, the woods! God, how I love 'em!" He raised his arms to the stars like a Greek tragedian, took a few steps into the darkness and fell heavily over a tree root.

"Hope you didn't hurt yourself," said Reims, helping him to his feet. "Don't go walking where you can't see around here or you'll end in the bottom of a gulley." He helped them unload their baggage into the two cabins. "Now Mary and I are going to leave you and give you a chance to get some rest."

"I don't ever expect to wake up in this heavenly place," said Mrs. Robbins.

"Me, too," said Mrs. Weller. "I just want to sleep for three days."

"Exactly," said Tom Reims. "Breakfast is at seven-thirty. First bell at six forty-five."

The sun rose over the top of Saw Tooth Mountain and enveloped with its warming rays the group of log buildings known as the Bar Z Bar Ranch.

In one of the cabins Mr. Horace Robbins lay huddled under a mound of Turkey-red blankets. He was having an unpleasant dream in which he was driving an automobile at great speed down a pitch-dark road. He was frightfully drowsy, but his friend Mrs. Weller kept him awake with a big hand bell which she rang in his ear whenever he nodded.

He stirred protestingly under the blankets. Then he realized the bell was real. "Good gracious," said Mrs. Robbins from beneath a similar pile across the room. "Don't tell me that's the breakfast bell. We can't be late the first morning of all things."

"I thought we came out here to relax," said Mr. Robbins, burrowing deeper.

Mrs. Robbins was already out of bed and rummaging through a suitcase.

"Argue about that after breakfast," she said. "The main thing now is to get into some of these trick clothes. Oh, dear. What *do* you suppose they wear for breakfast?"

"As far as I'm concerned it doesn't make much difference," said Mr. Robbins, letting his feet hang over the edge of the bed. "I left everything home to make room for the Wellers' baggage."

Half an hour later he emerged from the cabin dressed in an old flannel shirt and a pair of blue jeans turned up halfway to his knees and so stiff with newness that they crackled when he walked. On his head was a huge straw hat. The sides of its flaring brim almost touched above the crown. A pair of obviously new high-heeled boots completed the costume.

He walked over to the Wellers' door, the boots causing him to totter on the rough ground. "Hi," he called.

The door flew open disclosing Mr. Weller wearing a brown Stetson with a brim like an umbrella, a Western shirt complete with yoke and pearl buttons, and blue jeans that fitted like a pair of Elizabethan long-hose.

"My God," said Mr. Robbins. "What time are you due on the lot?"

Mrs. Weller pushed her husband gently through the door and posed beside him in a pair of Bedford cord jodhpurs, a red scarf under the open collar of her shirt and a little three-cornered felt hat set jauntily on the back of her immaculately groomed head.

"Good morning, old man," said Mr. Weller, rubbing his hands together briskly. "All set for a prance on the pampas?"

Until a moment before Mr. Robbins had rather fancied himself as looking fairly authentic, based on amateur standards. The Wellers, however, suddenly made him feel like the clown who, in his boyhood days, used to ride a donkey at the end of circus parades.

He followed them dejectedly down the hill toward a large log building, presumably the mess hall. From its stone chimney the smoke of a wood fire rose through the still air.

They hesitated in front of the entrance. "I feel the way I did my first morning in boarding school," said Mrs. Robbins, adjusting the collar of her denim jacket nervously.

"Come, come, *mes enfants. En avant, en avant,*" cried Mr. Weller, seizing the latch of the big door. It stuck for a moment; then, as he pushed with his shoulder, it gave way with a crash, precipitating him into the mess hall.

Mr. Robbins was conscious of startled faces turned toward them as they stood huddled in the doorway, of a great fire burning at the end of the room and of three long tables from one of which Mary Reims was hurrying toward them.

"Good morning," she said. "I was beginning to think you'd gone home mad. But its your prerogative to be late the first morning. Now you're all at my table except Bobby. The children eat together at their own table. They call it the trough."

The news did not strike Bobby either favorably or humorously.

"I don't wanna eat with the children," he said.

Mr. Robbins, foreseeing a violent scene as his introduction to the Bar Z Bar Ranch, resisted a desire to turn and rush out of the mess hall. "Perhaps," he suggested, "just this morning . . ."

"Nonsense," said Mary Reims. To their amazement she took Bobby firmly by the arm and had him seated at the trough before he could dramatize a suitable protest. He sat with lowered head, scowling at his plate, while his future companions examined him skeptically.

"There," said Mary Reims, returning. "He's happy as a clam. Now I've saved four places for you right around me. Let me introduce you to a few of your fellow sufferers. That doleful-looking wreck next to you is Hank, generally known as Old Hank because that's just what he is. He's our head wrangler. And next to

him are Mr. and Mrs. Poindexter, and that's Slim, our second mate. And Mr. and Mrs. Perkins, and Mrs. Trilling, and our fisherman, Mr. Briscoe." She went around the table.

"Do you fish?" asked Mr. Briscoe.

Mr. Robbins said he had brought some equipment but he certainly was no fisherman. Briscoe lost interest.

"You're a horseman," said Mr. Perkins, approvingly.

"Why anyone wants to fish when they can ride is too much for me."

Mr. Robbins had to admit he was no great shakes with horses, either. The Perkinses and Mr. Briscoe looked puzzled.

"Do you write?" asked Mrs. Poindexter hopefully.

Mr. Robbins said he did not. Mrs. Poindexter looked disappointed. "That's too bad," she said. "We've had some very interesting writers at the Bar Z Bar. Graham Wood was here last summer. He finished *Purple Hills* right in your cabin. You've read it, of course."

Mr. Robbins had not. Mrs. Poindexter appeared dumbfounded and resumed her attack on a large pile of griddle cakes.

Mary Reims rapped on her glass. "Now who'd like to take the luncheon ride today and who wants to go just for the morning?"

"I think," Mr. Weller said, "that this being our first day Mrs. Weller and I will take a canter by ourselves. Just an hour or two of brisk riding to get unlimbered."

"Oh, you five will go off by yourselves today with Old Hank," said Mary Reims. "Mostly walking. We've got to get you fitted to your horses."

Mr. Weller opened his mouth as if to speak, then, catching Mrs. Weller's eye, he remained silent.

Down at the corral the horses were saddled and waiting for their riders. They stood with drooping heads at a log rail, obviously asleep.

Old Hank approached. "This here one's yours," he said to Mr. Robbins, landing a resounding thwack on the rump of a huge buckskin mare. "Name's Dolly. Good hoss. Your party's goin' out first. Mount up any time."

Mr. Robbins approached Dolly hesitantly from the rear, with a view to moving in on her left side. Dolly countered by placing her rump firmly against that of the horse on her left. Turning her head she cast a hostile eye on her new tormenter. Mr. Robbins shrugged and started to go in on the right, but with a graceful posterior shift Dolly blocked that move also and took in Mr. Robbins with her other eye.

Mr. Robbins walked around the end of the hitching rail to make a frontal attack. "Good Dolly," he said, crouching to go under the rail. Dolly snorted and threw her head back, her eyes distended with horror.

"Hey, don't go at 'em from there," said Old Hank. "Go in from in back."

Mr. Robbins resumed his original position and, waiting until Dolly and her pals had apparently gone

to sleep again, lunged apprehensively between them.

"Hello, old hoss," he said ingratiatingly, running an uncertain hand over Dolly's soft muzzle. Dolly showed the whites of her eyes and, raising her head, brought it sharply down on Mr. Robbins' straw hat.

"Oh, to hell with you," said Mr. Robbins, but Dolly was already on her way back to sleep and did not seem to resent it.

"All right, you can mount up any time," called Old Hank.

Mr. Weller untied his horse and started to mount. "Heigh-ho Silver!" he cried.

"Hey," called Old Hank, "don't mount at the rail. Lead 'em out where it's open."

Mr. Weller, half up, came back to earth. He was saying something, but it was lost in the clop of hoofs on the hard-baked ground.

Forewarned, Mr. Robbins led Dolly away from the rail. She towered above him like a tawny mountain. He made an unsuccessful attempt to insert his left foot in the stirrup. What did they think he was? One of the Rockettes? By grasping the pommel with his right hand and leaning backward as far as possible he was finally able to insert his toe in the stirrup with the aid of his left hand. He thought he felt his pelvis crack, but he was not going to admit defeat if his whole framework came apart. He made one or two ineffectual hops from his right foot. With his leg anchored in mid-air he was like a man who has placed one foot on the mantelpiece and is now expected to jump up on it from that position.

Old Hank, ever alert for incompetence, came rush-

ing to the rescue. Seizing Mr. Robbins by the ample
slack of his blue jeans he hurled him into the saddle.
"Up you go, Pop," he said cheerily. An immense de-
pression settled over Mr. Robbins.

"You'll catch on in a few days," said Mr. Weller,
reassuringly. "Just out of condition, that's all."

Old Hank, mounting his own horse with one quick,
effortless movement, surveyed his charges without en-
thusiasm. "O.K.," he said. "Let's go."

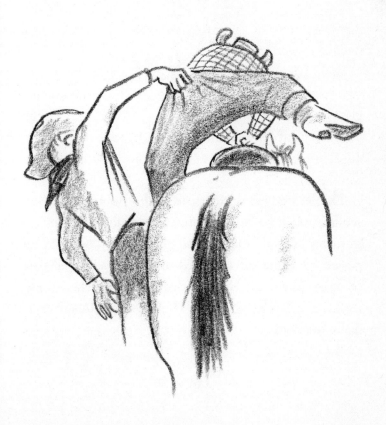

Bobby trudged up the road to the Robbinses' cabin, scuffing up little puffs of dust. Gone the department-store cowboy suit and the two guns. They had been replaced by a carefully battered black hat, a stained pair of blue jeans and high-heeled boots which already looked as dilapidated as Old Hank's. Mrs. Robbins put down her book.

"Bobby, dear, I haven't seen you all day. What *have* you been doing?"

"Nothing."

"Tell me, dear, how are you getting on with your riding? You always go out after we do."

"O.K."

"Have you trotted yet?"

"Oh, sure."

"Don't tell me you've cantered, too?"

"Oh, sure."

"But Bobby, a week ago you'd never been on a horse. You *will* be careful, won't you, dear?"

"Oh, sure." Bobby picked up a baseball glove from the corner of the porch. "I gotta go now, Gram."

"It's a great pleasure to see you, Bobby," said Mr. Robbins. "Thank you for looking us up."

But Bobby had no time for persiflage. He was already hurrying down the road toward the corral.

"He seems to be having a good time," said Mrs. Robbins, doubtfully.

"I don't know how you tell," said Mr. Robbins. "We never see him." His summer of companionship with his grandson wasn't working out just as he had planned it, but perhaps what appeared to be happening was more important.

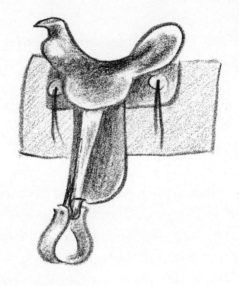

Mary Reims was making her rounds of the breakfast tables with her morning riding lists. "This morning," she said, "Slim is taking out an all-day ride to High Rim." She hovered over the Perkinses. "Bee and Sam will want to go on that, won't you? You like the hard ones. You'll have to start at eight-thirty."

"Wonderful," said the Perkinses, trying not to look smug.

"I've put down the Barnums for High Rim, too,"

said Mary. "I hope it isn't going to be too much for you."

"Not us," said the Barnums, obviously flattered.

"Good. And how about the Trimbles? Think you can take High Rim?"

The Trimbles were sure they could.

"O.K. That's that. And now for Robbins, Weller and Company. You're graduating today to a regular ride."

"High Rim sounds good to me," said Mr. Weller.

"Oh, not yet, George. I have you and Horace and Jane and Sally down for a lovely lunch ride up Paradise Creek. Incidentally you're going to see some beautiful mountain wild flowers. Mrs. Trilling is going. She's a walking encyclopedia on mountain flowers."

Mrs. Trilling lowered her eyes modestly. "There are *some* I don't know," she said.

"I spent a year in the saddle on the Mexican border," said Mr. Weller to Mrs. Poindexter on his left. "I really don't see why I have to take flower rides. . . ."

"I *love* flowers," said Mrs. Poindexter. "I'm going with you today just because of them. Usually I take walks and paint them."

The luncheon ride took off up the slopes of a mountain behind the ranch, twisting through a forest of lodgepole pine whose floor was littered, like a child's jack-straw game, with the silver-gray trunks of long-fallen trees. Eventually they emerged onto a mountain meadow carpeted with multicolored wild flowers.

Dolly, obviously no mean flower lover herself, immediately began snatching greedily to the right and left seizing great mouthfuls of delphinium and purple lupin which she carried on either side of her mouth like an equine bridesmaid until they gradually disappeared between her rubbery lips.

Mrs. Poindexter was riding immediately behind Mr. Robbins. "Letting your horse eat on the trail is one of the seven deadly sins," she said, archly.

"Thank you," said Mr. Robbins, yanking at the astonished Dolly as she dove for a fresh supply of flowers. It didn't seem to him that it was any of Mrs. Poindexter's business if he let Dolly eat until she had a stroke, but this was his first regular ride and he didn't want to get into an argument.

An hour later they stopped beside a brook, ice cold from the snow fields above. "This is where we eat," said Old Hank. He turned to Mr. Weller, who had been riding right behind him. "Here, I'll give you a hand loosening your cinch."

"Not me," said Mr. Weller. "I used to do this half a dozen times a day."

"That so?" said Old Hank without interest.

"Cavalry," said Mr. Weller. "First, New York."

Old Hank spat carefully, moved over to a clump of trees and began to unload the pack mule.

"Going to build a fire?" asked Mr. Weller.

Old Hank nodded. "I'll help you," said Mr. Weller.

"No need," said Old Hank, but Mr. Weller was already headed for the woods. He returned dragging a great pile of branches. These he broke up carefully and laid a fire in the shape of a wigwam. When Old Hank had finished unpacking the mule he swept it aside impatiently and built a fire of his own.

In the effortless way of one who has gone through the routine a thousand times, Old Hank produced steaks, peas, hot bread, coffee and apricots in less time than it would have taken Mr. Robbins to scramble eggs on his stove at home. The latter watched him admiringly. "Can't I help you clean up?" he asked.

"Naw," said Old Hank. "I just throw everything in this bag. Get washed at the ranch."

Nothing seemed hard to Old Hank. He squatted under a tree, placed a blade of grass between his teeth and watched a fat cloud travel across the blue sky. Mr. Robbins sat down beside him. They observed the cloud in silence.

"Gosh, you're lucky," said Mr. Robbins, finally. "You get money for doing what I travel thousands of miles and pay through the nose to do."

Old Hank looked at him in astonishment. "What's lucky about this?" he asked. "Nothin' but mountains an' trees an' hosses."

"Don't you like horses?" asked Mr. Robbins.

Old Hank looked at him again as if to make sure that this was not some new form of intellectual leg-pulling. One couldn't trust dudes. "Hosses?" he said incredulously. Failing to produce words which would adequately express his feelings he spat forcibly over his shoulder into the pine needles.

"But think what a wonderful life you've had. Out-doors all the time."

"Who wants to live outdoors all the time?" said Old Hank. "Either too cold or too hot or rainin'. No, I'll tell you. If I had it to do all over again I'd get me a little rest'rant. There's a life. Standin' inside all day by a nice warm stove, plenty to eat an' no hosses nor mules."

Mr. Robbins pondered this conversation as they rode home. It upset him, somehow. He watched Old Hank, at the head of the line, riding as if he were the upper half of a centaur.

In spite of his age and his stringy body, he gave an impression of latent strength. Toughness was per-haps a better word—the kind of toughness that you knew would enable him to meet any contingency that might arise without the expenditure of an ounce of superfluous energy.

He had an intangible quality that comes only from belonging; a quality which he shared with the elk and the moose and the little animals that burrow under the earth and along the banks of the streams and which enables the delicate branches of the balsam to bend before the winter winds and resume their symmetry when the storm is passed.

Mr. Robbins found himself comparing Old Hank with Mr. Weller, who was riding just behind him.

"Kind of boring just walking up- and downhill," said Mr. Weller. "Wish that old goat would let us run them a little."

"Why don't you ask him if you can lead a charge?" suggested Mr. Robbins.

The trail curved around the end of a great fallen tree. It had been stricken decades before and now it lay like a skeleton, its branches white and brittle against the green of the forest floor.

Suddenly Mr. Robbins heard a noise behind him as if someone had set off a package of giant firecrackers. He turned quickly to see Mr. Weller struggling to extricate his foot from the dry upper branches of the tree. His horse, which had been dreaming of upland pastures, being suddenly awakened by a series of unexplained explosions, chose to remove her body from the point of danger as rapidly as possible. There being a horse in front and another behind, she did the only thing possible and leaped sideways.

In doing so, however, she failed to take Mr. Weller's body with her, largely because it was still attached to the tree. At the moment that Mr. Robbins turned it was poised in mid-air above the trail, looking for all the world like an advanced case of levitation.

This interesting phenomenon could not endure for long, however, and an instant later Mr. Robbins beheld his friend lying on the ground, blinking at the treetops and the blue sky.

Directly behind him, Mrs. Poindexter was doubled up with merriment. "Excuse me for laughing," she said, "but you must agree that was very, very funny. Have you, by any chance, ever read *The Adventures of an Irish R. M.?*"

Old Hank came trotting back over the fallen tree trunks. "Fall off?" he asked.

Mr. Weller sat up stiffly. "That's a vicious horse," he said. "I've had horses buck with me and I've had them rear, but this one did both at the same time."

Mr. Weller's horse was chewing on a large bunch of lupin a few feet away. She looked at him with accusing brown eyes. "You all right?" asked Old Hank.

"If you mean have I broken my neck—no."

"O.K., let's go," said Old Hank.

They reached the foot of the mountain and emerged from the woods into a broad valley. The trail wound through the sagebrush like a meadow brook.

Old Hank set off at a brisk trot, his body glued to his saddle. Mr. Robbins, watching enviously, concluded that Old Hank's horse must be built differently than Dolly. As the pace became brisker he felt as if he were seated on an inverted pile driver. One might as well try to sit tight on a kangaroo.

He tried posting, but the stirrups were so long that after rising once or twice his feet slid into them to his boot heels. Eventually he evolved a compromise—post twice, then bang, bang, bang, post, post, bang, bang, bang!

Old Hank broke into a canter as one shifts smoothly into high gear. Dolly merely lengthened her stride and continued to trot. Post, bang, post, bang-bang, bang-bang. Mr. Robbins' backbone was being pounded into the base of his brain. He yanked at the reins in a frantic

attempt to make Dolly canter. She was a horse that
evidently wanted to please for she responded with
something that was half trot and half canter. Even
in his agony Mr. Robbins almost fell off trying to see

whether she was cantering with her front feet and trotting with her back, or vice versa.

The canter extended into a gallop. Dolly was forced unwillingly to abandon the trot, but her new gait still bore no resemblance to that of Old Hank's horse. To Mr. Robbins it seemed more like a workout in a camel corps.

His left hand, flailing the air, came into contact with the horn of the saddle and closed on it with a viselike grip. It wasn't cricket, of course, but who was going to see him? Then his right hand came up unconsciously and joined his left. With his arms he pulled himself into a half-standing position and was suddenly filled with great exhilaration. He felt like the back man in a chariot, clinging to the driver's belt as they flew over the rough ground. He should have a toga billowing out behind him.

"Caramba!" he shouted. Clutching the saddle horn more tightly with his left hand he belted Dolly between the ears with the end of his reins.

Mrs. Robbins stood in front of her cabin mirror, trying her new Western hat at various angles. Like Mr. Robbins' it was a big straw affair with high, curling side brims, only hers was tied under her chin with a leather thong and she usually wore it between her shoulder blades.

Styles were changing even in the West, which traditionally resists change. Gone the high-crowned Stetsons of Remington and Russell, the broad flapping chaps, worn grease-shiny with smoke and dirt and sweat, the roweled spurs. The East had come, eager to succumb to the West, but there were indications that the West was unconsciously succumbing, on at least a fifty-fifty basis, to the East.

The result, as far as dudes were concerned at least, was a curious hybrid costume containing elements of Sheridan and Cody, Abercrombie and Fitch, Brooks Brothers, Billings, Nantucket, Jamaica, Three Forks, Sears, Roebuck and Hobe Sound.

The Wellers wore their costumes from morning until bedtime, but Mr. Robbins could never reconcile himself to the harshness of blue jeans against his unaccustomed legs or the feeling which his high-heeled boots always gave him that he was standing on two sticks of kindling wood. As a result a good part of his day was spent like a debutante in changing his clothes.

He liked to go down to the corral before the rides started and watch the wranglers cut the horses out of the milling, kicking groups and throw on the heavy saddles with an economy of motion that reduced him to a state of hopeless envy.

These lithe, hipless young men fascinated him. They were all alike, yet all so different. Each wore his hat and his clothes in a fashion that was his alone and that made him quickly recognizable a quarter of a mile away. Each rode differently. Each walked differently. And yet, although each one was an uncompromising individualist, they belonged to a world of horses and cattle and mountains which left a common imprint on them all, marking them as men of the West in a manner that no Easterner could ever hope to imitate.

Occasionally, as Mr. Robbins sat on the step of the saddle room or leaned against its rough, sunbaked wall, chatting with these carefree youths who rode through life with such sure and graceful balance, untroubled by tomorrow or the consequences of today, absorbed in the moment because they were physically prepared to meet whatever it brought—occasionally, at such times, he would forget his age and his thirty-six-inch waistline. His baggy, turned-up blue jeans would suddenly fit him like Slim's. He would pull his straw hat down over his nose like Old Hank and his blood would quicken with the desire to mount with the latter's easy grace, to break into a lope as his body hit the saddle.

Perhaps that was why Easterners came to the West.

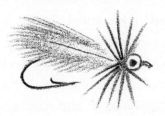

"Walch and I are going to do the Beaver Tail," said Mr. Briscoe at breakfast.

Mr. Robbins looked at them doubtfully, half expecting to see them break into some kind of dance step. You never could tell what was going to happen at a dude ranch.

"We're going to fish up the Beaver Tail from where it runs into Cat Creek," said Mr. Briscoe, as if this explained everything.

"Want to come along?" asked Mr. Briscoe.

"But I really don't know anything about fishing," said Mr. Robbins.

"We'll show you," said Mr. Walch.

They left their car beside the highway and walked for miles along a rough path. A stream flowed snake-like through a marshy meadow on their right.

"This is the spot," said Mr. Briscoe finally, setting down his rod and boots under a tree.

"The exact place," said Mr. Walch.

Mr. Robbins could see no difference between where they were and where they had been for the last hour and a half. He sat down on the grass willingly enough, however, glad at least that he would not have to carry his waders any further.

"What kind of fly will we start him out with?" said Mr. Walch.

"I'd thought I'd try him with a Black Hackle," said Mr. Briscoe. They talked as if Mr. Robbins were a horse.

"In this light!" cried Mr. Briscoe. "That's crazy. Here, let him try this Number Six Grackle. They'll fight for it."

"You couldn't catch a cold with those things," said Mr. Walch contemptuously. Mr. Robbins leaned back against the tree and closed his eyes. He hoped they would go on arguing all day and let him rest.

"I'll tell you," said Mr. Walch. "We'll start him with a Royal Wolf. Any boob can catch fish with one of those." He addressed Mr. Robbins directly for the first time. "Watch how I tie the fly on so you'll know how to do it. Pass the leader through the eye of the hook like that. See? Make a loop, pass the end over and under—there. Think you could do it now? Here. Stick those extra flies in your hat. If one doesn't work, try another."

Mr. Robbins took the rod, vowing never to remove the Royal Wolf from his leader even though it proved to be anathema to every trout in the West.

"I'm fishing upstream," said Mr. Briscoe.

"O.K. I'll fish down," said Mr. Walch.

That seemed to leave the section of stream directly in front of them to Mr. Robbins. Anything which involved a minimum of walking was all right with him.

"Let me give you a few pointers on casting," said Mr. Walch. They crossed the marshy hummocks to the edge of the Beaver Tail. Mr. Walch cast nonchalantly upstream, downstream and across. "See that little pool over there?" he said, laying the Royal Wolf neatly in the middle of it. "That's the kind of a place they hide out. Well, now you've got the idea. Hope you catch a million."

He strode away, whistling. Mr. Robbins was suddenly alone. The little stream corkscrewed its gurgling way through the meadow. All about him were gray-blue mountains. A killdeer flew back and forth protesting Mr. Robbins' presence with angry peeps. The rest of the world was wrapped in silence.

He tried a cast. Not so bad. At least it landed in the stream. As he whipped the line out he shuddered at the nearness of the hook to his face. Fine note to plant a hook in his eye out in this wilderness. Not the sort of thing you wanted to find in your eye wherever you might be.

He cast again. Oops! The Royal Wolf was wound around the stem of a wild carrot behind him. Laying the rod down he followed the line back with his fingers and disentangled it. He glanced about to see if Briscoe

or Walch were looking, but they had disappeared from sight. He wondered if they might have lain down in the long grass and gone to sleep. Perhaps that was the charm of fishing. He toyed with the idea but basically he was too conscientious.

He cast again with such excellent results, as far as distance was concerned, that his fly cleared the stream by several feet and anchored itself in the sagebrush on the opposite side. He crossed the slippery stones cautiously and disentangled it.

No use going back. One side was as good—or as bad— as the other. He started to walk upstream, stepped off

a hummock and found his right leg embedded in a deep pothole. His left leg remained, miraculously, on the hummock. There was no question in Mr. Robbins' mind that this time he had split his pelvis for keeps. What Dolly had started nature had finished. Why was the West so hostile to the pelvis?

The leg which had remained above ground was twisted in such a way that he could not move it. He raised himself on his arms, but was unable to see over the top of the grass. This was *it!* No one would ever find him here. In the spring some chance fisherman might stumble on his skeleton. Might even join it in the pothole.

He turned his body slowly and discovered to his surprise that, by lying face down, he could straighten out the surface leg. He did so and then pulled his other slowly and painfully from the muddy hole. He lay in the grass for a long time resting. He had never realized that fishing was so complicated.

Some old, atavistic hunting urge eventually drove him back to the edge of the stream. Vainly, without hope, he hurled the Royal Wolf at the swiftly flowing water until, through its burbling, he thought he could detect a mocking laugh.

He remembered that Walch and Briscoe had said that trout were the cagiest fish in the world. Let a fisherman, they declared, permit so much as his shadow to fall across the water or let him show his head and shoulders above the bank and all local fish would merely leer and go back to sleep beneath their stones.

That, of course, was why he wasn't catching anything. In his efforts to keep the Royal Wolf in the water rather than the sagebrush, he had made a spectacle of himself before every trout in the Beaver Tail.

He moved back from the bank to a point where a trout would have to use a periscope to see him. Then he walked down the stream several hundred yards to an area where presumably no fish would be apt to have heard of him. Once more he approached the stream until he could almost see the water.

This was the precise point, apparently, from which one should fish, but who in the world had ever heard of anyone casting over twenty-five feet of dry land? In the pictures on the covers of sporting-goods catalogues, fishermen always stood waist deep in the middle of the stream where every trout in the neighborhood was free to come up and take a good look.

There must be some other way. He tried approaching the bank on his knees, but even by this undignified method he could get no nearer than ten or fifteen feet without exposing himself.

Suppose he was starving. In the wilds the hunter,

to survive, must pit his intelligence against the instinct of the beast. He looked quickly up and down the stream to make sure that Briscoe and Walch were not in sight. Then he pulled a long length of line off his reel, laid the pole on the ground beside him, and began to wriggle through the grass on his stomach with the Royal Wolf between his thumb and forefinger. At the edge of the stream he parted the grass carefully and let the fly down to the surface of the water three feet below.

He watched it float down with the current. Then he pulled it slowly back, admiring the V of water which it created. How could any trout resist it?

He let out more line. His hook was swept beneath the bank and snagged. He stood up. To hell with the trout. Let them look if they wanted.

Tweaking on the line only seemed to anchor it more firmly under the bank. He might cut it, of course, but that would mean tying on a new fly. Remembering Mr. Walch's complex instructions, he resolved to do this only as a last resort.

He lay on his stomach and leaned over as far as he could. He could see the hook caught under a root but his hand was still a foot away from it. Inch by inch he worked forward and downward until he had the Royal Wolf in his fingers. He freed it—and then discovered that he was hanging so far over the edge of the bank he could not get back.

Should he give up the struggle and allow himself to slide, head first, into the stream? A few inches from his nose the Royal Wolf waited to impale him. He reflected that if it did he would be the first thing it had ever impaled or probably ever would.

A shadow fell across the water below him. In spite of his position his first thought was in criticism of the fisherman who was disclosing himself so carelessly. He heard Walch's voice. "For heaven's sake, Horace, I wondered whose legs those were. Here, let me give you a hand." Seizing Mr. Robbins by the feet he pulled

him up over the muddy edge of the bank onto the safety of the grass.

For a moment Mr. Robbins lay quite still. He could never live this down. He was not even sure he wanted to try. Far better had he remained in the pothole or slid quietly into the stream.

To his amazement Mr. Walch paid no further attention to the incident. "Look at that," he said, holding out his creel, bulging with fish. "Five big ones and I threw about ten little fellows back. There's Briscoe coming in. Let's call it a day and listen to his hard-luck stories."

Far up the meadow Mr. Briscoe was struggling across the hummocks. He held up his creel indicating, by gestures, its great weight. "By the way," said Mr. Walch

to Mr. Robbins, "how did you do?"

"Threw them all back," said Mr. Robbins.

Mr. Walch nodded absently. "Doesn't matter. We've got plenty."

They met at the tree where they had left their gear. Mr. Briscoe and Mr. Walch began immediately to rehearse their experiences. Neither evidenced the slightest interest in the exploits of the other. They continued to talk on the long walk back to the car.

Mr. Robbins felt the need to re-establish himself as one of the party. "I remember a day off Martha's Vineyard," he offered. "We were after blues. All of a sudden—"

"That upper pool—oh boy!" said Mr. Briscoe.

Mr. Robbins plodded down the path in silence.

Mrs. Taylor was the latest addition to the Bar Z Bar. She had a husband somewhere, but nobody seemed to know what she had done with him and none of the male guests cared much as long as he didn't show up, for Mrs. Taylor was a very pretty woman.

She sat beside Mr. Robbins at breakfast. "Are you going to the square dance at the Circle K tonight?" she asked.

Mr. Robbins said that he had never done any square dancing. The longer he stayed at the Bar Z Bar the more it became apparent that during a long and busy life he had never done anything.

"Oh, nonsense," said Mrs. Taylor. "You don't need to *know* square dancing. You just wade in and push around. Of course you're coming. We need you. Look here, I'm having some people for cocktails at the cabin tonight. You and Mrs. Robbins drop over and we'll talk about it."

When he had first begun to plan the trip to the ranch Mr. Robbins had gone to his old friend and family doctor, Joe Brennan, for a physical checkup. Joe had listened to his chest and taken his blood pressure and glanced casually down his throat, all the while discussing the future of the stock market, a routine that he had been following for twenty years. As Mr. Robbins was leaving his office, Joe had remarked as an afterthought that he was sound as a nut, but to remember his age. He was going into high country and he shouldn't jump around too much and if Mr. Robbins could find out about Tyrolean Oil give him a ring.

"Why don't we go and watch the kids?" said Mrs. Robbins when the matter of the square dance came up. "I'd like to see what Bobby does."

"It's about the only chance you'll have," said Mr. Robbins.

Mrs. Taylor's party was a wow. Long before it was

over the square dance at the Circle K was taken for granted.

When they arrived, the floor of the big barn was already crowded with characters from up and down the valley. The caller was announcing a new dance.

"Picking up Pawpaws!" cried Mrs. Taylor. *"Anybody* can do that. Just stand with me behind this couple and watch what they do."

She was right. "Picking up Pawpaws" was a dance that could be mastered at a low intellectual level. It consisted largely of a nonstop chase around the huge barn in pursuit of various young women. "Come on, boys, let's go find her," sang the chorus. The spirit of Pan began to stir in Mr. Robbins' veins so vigorously

that they were protruding around his temples. Round and round he raced, his breath coming in short, stabbing sobs. He found himself raising his knees as he ran and if he had had a reed pipe he would have played it with his final gasps.

The music stopped. He leaned weakly against a side beam. "You were wonderful," said Mrs. Taylor.

"Will you do the next with me?" said a tall young girl that Mr. Robbins could not remember ever having seen before. "I think it's 'Little Brown Jug.'" Mr. Robbins, unable to speak as yet, mopped his streaming face and nodded happily.

She could easily have been his daughter. In fact, granting a degree of precociousness on his part, she might even have qualified as his granddaughter. She also had lovely golden hair and a cute snub nose.

"I don't know it," he managed to gasp. Why did older people have to blow like grampuses whenever they moved around?

"Don't worry. I'll teach you," said the girl. It seemed to him that everyone was teaching him these days. "This is an easy one," she said. "Look. I'll show you."

It did seem fairly simple. Point your toe a couple of times. Slide a bit. A lot of hand slapping and eventually you were faced with a new partner. Mr. Robbins was disappointed by this last discovery. The music started and quickly grew faster. Again his breath left him and he could no longer make little pleasantries to his ever-changing partners. His whole effort was concentrated now on keeping his agony from showing on his face.

This was *it*. After all these years time was going to be called on him on the floor of a strange barn. What difference did it make whether it was strange or whether he'd been born in the place? The music would stop. They would gather round him with bowed heads and Mrs. Taylor and the little girl with the snub nose would say, "He was wonderful."

"Little brown jug," slap, slap, slap. Slide, slide. A lovely child in faded blue jeans was dancing opposite him with effortless grace. He tried to match her nonchalance, but as well expect nonchalance from a fish gasping out its life on a river bank. "You're wonderful," she smiled, and passed on down the line.

The music stopped. "You're red as a lobster," said Mrs. Robbins, anxiously. "Who in the world do you think you are? Fred Astaire? You'll have a stroke if you go on like that."

Mr. Robbins gave her an uncomprehending stare. "Want to do the next one with me?" he asked.

"But I don't know how."

"I'll teach you," said Mr. Robbins.

93

"I don't know what's gotten into Bobby," said Mrs. Robbins. "I hardly ever see him, and when I do, I don't know what he's talking about."

"I must get hold of the child," said Mr. Robbins. "I'd planned to teach him to fish and to do all sorts of things with him. Now we've been here for weeks and we haven't done a thing together. What in the world is he up to all day?"

"We ought to take him to Yellowstone Park some Sunday. We talked enough about it last spring. At least that's something we can do with him."

"We'll go next Sunday," said Mr. Robbins, decisively. "You invite a couple of his friends to go along and that doesn't mean the Wellers."

Mr. and Mrs. Robbins were not the first parents, or grandparents, at the Bar Z Bar to become conscious of the disappearance of their offspring. The junior group not only ate together, but lived a life apart from the time they arose until they went to bed at night. They rode together, they square danced together, they sat together around the red bottle cooler in their off-horse moments, affecting extreme exhaustion, pouring soft drinks into their slim bodies and discussing a world from which adults were uncompromisingly excluded.

94

Although they worshiped at the altar of non conformity they lived under a caste system divided into two sharply defined groups and governed by codes as rigid as those of any monastic order.

The upper echelon, ranging from thirteen to nineteen, was generally known as the Jet Set. Their life was an alternating current shuttling between high adventure and insufferable boredom. Françoise Sagan and

Pamela Moore were their oracles. They carried paper-bound copies of their works in the back pockets of their blue jeans which could be taken out and read during the unendurable periods when the horses were forced to walk.

The relationship between the Jet Set and the older world was one of haughty indifference. All persons over twenty-five years of age were obviously either cubes or fuds—hopeless, helpless souls who had lost

touch with present-day realities and were rattling down the chute to oblivion without having the foggiest idea of what was going on.

The acolytes of this hierarchy were recruited from the ranks of those under twelve. As a group they were still frankly and unashamedly children who spent their waking moments, when not riding, eating or drinking, in pushing one another around in front of the mess hall. Their common denominator with the Jet Set was their uncompromising attitude toward adults. Both groups lived in a world surrounded by "No Admission" signs. It was into this latter fraternity that Bobby had disappeared as completely as if he had jumped into a magic lake whose clear waters revealed his actions to those above but cut him off in all other respects from his former life.

He did not appear to consciously evade his grandparents. It was merely that their paths did not often cross. When he met them during the day he was polite, as a young stranger should be to an aged and somewhat helpless couple. He preferred walking to breakfast alone and at night he put himself to bed at more or less the right time, not so much because he wanted to, but because it was the only way to avoid the humiliating hand of authority.

On the following Sunday the Robbinses' station wagon left for Yellowstone Park immediately after breakfast. In it were Mr. and Mrs. Robbins, Bobby, and his new and inseparable friends, Bink and Beany Perkins.

In spite of the fact that the Yellowstone is a sight-seers' Mecca, the attitude of the departing group was somewhat less than enthusiastic. Years before Mr. and Mrs. Robbins had inspected every steaming pool and bubbling mudhole in the area and, as for Bobby, he could not understand why anyone would voluntarily leave a place like the ranch just to go and look at something.

"But Bobby, you wouldn't want to go home without seeing Old Faithful, would you?"

"Why not? I know what it looks like from the pictures. You don't want me to miss the softball game do you, Gram?"

"We can take a couple of your friends. We'll ask the Perkins boys."

"Oh, Gram, they wouldn't want to take a trip like *that*. It would be awful embarrassing to ask fellows like that."

Whether or not it embarrassed the Perkins boys their parents, at least, jumped at the opportunity.

"We've been putting it off and off," said Mrs. Perkins. "Sam's terrible about such things. He won't miss his riding so we can't go on weekdays and on Sundays he says he'd just as soon take a bicycle ride on the Merritt Parkway."

Regardless of the pressures which caused them to be present, the Perkins boys had been coached into a state of excessive politeness. They competed with one another for the privilege of opening the car doors for Mr. and Mrs. Robbins, or of carrying small objects for them, and they never addressed a remark to Mr. Robbins without prefacing it with "sir."

This Chesterfieldian atmosphere distressed Bobby no end, for he knew only too well that it was going to involve him eventually in comparisons in which he was sure to be the loser.

"You don't have to be so polite all the time," he assured his friends. "They're only my grandfather and my grandmother."

Left to their own devices on the rear seat the Perkins boys seemed to find it easy to relax. They did this by pommeling each other and emitting shrill cries which eventually caused them to go into uncontrollable paroxysms of laughter.

After listening to this routine for an hour or so Mr. Robbins' nerves began to give.

99

"Now if you boys will be quiet instead of yelling in that asinine way all the time," he said, as they entered the park, "we might see a bear."

Beany Perkins disentangled himself from his two companions. "Sir," he said, "are they wild?"

"Very," said Mr. Robbins.

The boys spent several miles discussing what they would do to a wild bear if they encountered one in the middle of a forest emptyhanded. At that moment they rounded a corner and almost ran into a jam of stalled cars that completely blocked the road.

"Oh, oh," said Mr. Robbins, jamming on his brakes, "looks like an accident."

"Bear," shouted the three boys simultaneously.

"Everyone close your windows," cried Mrs. Robbins. "And don't get out of the car."

Two black bears were making the rounds of the stalled cars, standing on their hind legs and sticking their heads through the open windows like customs inspectors. Following them were a group of people with cameras glued to their eyes, while small children peered between them and laid down a barrage of popcorn, chocolate, tinfoil, chewing gum, broken cookies and an occasional piece of bark.

The boys started to get out. "No, no, boys. Don't you see that sign on the tree? 'Under no circumstances are people to feed bears or leave their cars to photograph them.'"

"What are all these people doing, then?" asked Bobby.

"They are very stupid people," said Mr. Robbins. "Those bears may turn on them and tear somebody to pieces any minute."

"Let's stay and watch them," said Bobby.

"No," said Mr. Robbins. "We've got to get to the geyser country."

"Bink has to go to the bathroom," said Bobby.

"Well, he'll have to wait, dear, until we get to a place," said Mrs. Robbins.

They worked their way through the road block and proceeded on their way. Before they had gone a mile they ran into another jam.

"Gracious," said Mr. Robbins, bringing the car to a stop. "This must be some kind of a bear festival." The attraction in this instance was three black bears who were trying to climb into the open back end of a station wagon from which some little girls were throwing out food. The onlookers took pictures eagerly. "Aren't they cute?" said a stout woman in a visor cap to Mrs. Robbins.

"Let's wait," said Bobby, "and see what happens if they get in."

"I wouldn't want to see it," said Mr. Robbins. "Besides, we're late."

"What to?" asked Bobby.

"I don't know," said Mr. Robbins, crossly. "But if we keep running into bear jams it'll take us a week to get through this place."

They pushed on past lone bears, sitting disconsolately beside the road like pitchmen who have failed to attract a crowd. Clouds of steam rose above the trees on their right.

"Look, boys, the geysers," cried Mrs. Robbins. But the boys had resumed their never-ending pastime of mauling one another and had no time for the wonders of nature.

"Now see here, boys," said Mr. Robbins, sternly, "just cut that stuff and pay attention. I'm darned if I'm going to lug you halfway across the state to see something like this and have you spend all your time sitting on each other and yelling."

"Yes, sir," said the Perkins boys, sitting up immediately and looking alert.

"We'll get out here and see the geysers," said Mrs. Robbins. "That will give everyone a chance to stretch their legs. And remember, boys, you mustn't go off the boardwalk. This is just a thin crust and there are great fires underneath it. You'd go right through if you tried to walk on it." The boys were impressed and tiptoed gingerly down the crowded plank walk.

A young man in a Hawaiian shirt, draped with camera gear, crawled under the rail and tiptoed over the white-crusted surface to the outlet of one of the steaming pools, into which he inserted a hesitant finger. Behind him his bride squealed with anxious delight. "Ain't so hot," he announced. Using the butt end of a fountain pen he wrote his name carefully in the soft mud at the edge of the pool and returned to his admiring spouse.

"Why didn't he break through the crust and fall in the fire?" asked Bink.

"I don't know," said Mr. Robbins. "Wish he had."

"Horace, what a dreadful thing to say. Now we'll get back to the car and go to see the Devil's Paint Pot."

"Don't forget Bink has to go to the bathroom," said Bobby.

"Me, too," said Beany.

"Well, I don't see what you can do about it here," said Mrs. Robbins. "Maybe the thing to do is to skip the Devil's Paint Pot and go right through to Old Faithful just as quick as we can."

They tore down the road until, rounding a sharp corner, they almost ran into a mother bear, her three cubs and twenty-seven automobiles. The spaces between them and the road banks on either side were jammed with photographers, getting in the way of other photographers, and the air was filled with flying food.

"How cute," said Mrs. Robbins. "Let's watch."

"No," said Mr. Robbins. "If Goldilocks was appearing with them in person I wouldn't stop now." He began to edge through the crowd of tourists, who glared and inquired of one another why people who were in such a hurry didn't stay home.

They sped down the road. "There's Old Faithful," cried Mrs. Robbins. "See it? It's that dome-shaped rock with all the people standing in front of it."

"I don't see what's so wonderful about it," said Bobby.

"It isn't spouting now, Bobby. It only spouts once an hour."

"Sir," screamed Bink. "There's a *place*. Over there on the left by the trees."

"Horace, why don't you pull into that parking lot in front of the hotel. Then you can go in and find out when Old Faithful's due to go off again and we'll meet you at the car."

"You'd better hurry back," said Mr. Robbins, "then we can go over and get a good spot."

He climbed the terrace steps of the hotel. The big lobby was empty except for a man and woman who were talking to the desk clerk.

"Excuse me for interrupting," said Mr. Robbins.

The woman glared at him over her shoulder and continued talking. "My husband and I love the Belair," she said. "We've been going there fifteen years. Isn't it fifteen, Jim?"

"Sixteen," said the man.

"But there was one year when Joel was sick and we didn't go. Don't you remember?"

"I've counted that," said the man.

"All I want to ask you—" said Mr. Robbins.

"Is there a convention going on or something?" asked the woman, moving in between Mr. Robbins and the desk clerk so that he could no longer catch the latter's eye. "Joel's our little boy," she said, resuming the conversation.

The desk clerk nodded sympathetically.

"He's twenty-two," said the man.

"Well, he wasn't twenty-two the year he was sick. That was back in 1944."

"Forty-five," said the man. "He was taken sick on V-J Day."

"He's married now. They have a lovely baby." The woman started to fumble in her handbag.

Mr. Robbins raised himself on his toes until he could see the desk clerk over the woman's shoulder. "When does Old Faithful go off again?" he shouted. The clerk frowned and pointed to the picture window in the front of the lobby. Glancing in the direction indicated, Mr. Robbins could see the jet of Old Faithful pushing higher and higher into the misty air. "It's been going four minutes," the clerk said.

"The nerve of some people," said the woman.

Mr. Robbins hurried out onto the deep veranda which commanded a view not only of Old Faithful but of the surrounding area. There was no sign of Mrs. Robbins and the three boys. Old Faithful was approaching its peak. Then he spotted them emerging from a log building on the edge of the parking lot.

He ran down the steps shouting, but they were too far away to hear. A few of the people on the veranda concluded that he must be a house detective pursuing one of the guests and came to the rail for a better view. Mr. Robbins ran down the asphalt drive in the direction of his family waving his arms and pointing, but they were all engrossed in eating something and did not notice him until he was a few feet away.

"Hurry," he panted. Old Faithful, having reached its maximum height, was definitely beginning to fall off.

"What in the world is the matter, Horace? Oh, look, boys, the thing has started."

"Run," said Mr. Robbins. "It's almost over."

"We can't run with ice cream cones," said Bobby. "The stuff'll fall out. We see it all right."

"I *do* think," said Mrs. Robbins, "that the best thing is to go to the car and watch it from there. Then perhaps, when it's all over, we can get out ahead of this awful crowd. Bobby, *please* don't let your ice cream drip all over your shirt."

Old Faithful slowly subsided. As the last steaming pulsation sank beneath the surface, the crowd around it broke up as if dispersed by tear gas and made a rush for the parking area. In five minutes the orderly rows of cars had been dispersed into a milling jam of people and automobiles, all struggling to get nowhere in particular as quickly as possible.

"When do we eat?" asked Bobby. A huge hard-top convertible had worked itself squarely across the road while attempting a U turn and was now unable to move in either direction. The blare of a hundred protesting horns rolled through the forest, reaching the indifferent ears of the moose and the black bear, the beaver and the gopher and all the live things of the wilderness that had long since become used to this sort of noise and merely regarded it as the harmless man call.

Through the confusion a mother bear and her three cubs threaded their way confidently beneath a rain of titbits. "Aren't we going to see any real bears?" asked Bobby.

But Mr. Robbins was blowing his horn at the hard-top and did not reply.

The days were piling up into weeks and the weeks were beginning to run together like spilled paints. It was becoming difficult to remember whether it was Monday or Friday and what one had done the day before yesterday. Grooves had been worn and time was slipping through them at an ever-increasing speed.

The moonlight night of their arrival seemed infinitely remote and this brought with it a certain sadness, for it meant that soon these mountains and pine forests, these upland meadows and swift streams would be memories, and New York, at the moment so remote, would be rumbling and roaring in their ears once more.

Mr. Robbins had become an Old-timer. He knew most of the trails and had taken all the long rides that marked one's coming of age at Bar Z Bar. He knew the names of the principal peaks, could tell a speckled trout from a cutthroat, and was able to tie a trout fly to his leader. He could loosen a cinch or tighten it without asking Slim or Old Hank if that was about right. He could ride twenty-five miles without feeling stiff and his jeans had long ceased to crackle with newness.

Above all, he had learned to know and to live with Dolly. His relationship to her was no longer romantic, but savored more of the mature understanding that comes of long association. For weeks he had tried to kindle in her stubborn and indifferent heart some spark of affection, some evidence of friendly recognition, but Dolly was an Old-timer herself. She knew that eventually Mr. Robbins would be replaced by some Mr. Smith, and Mr. Smith by a Mr. Jones—that they would all try their blandishments on her and that in the end they would all climb on her back and force her to carry them up every mountain in the neighborhood under the illusion that, by doing so, *they* were getting exercise.

From Dolly's point of view there was some reason for cynicism. She wanted none of this emotionalism and she tried in every way to indicate her feelings. When Mr. Robbins approached her at the hitching rail, making soft noises, she pretended to be asleep, and when he stroked the soft peach skin of her muzzle she threw her head up sharply, hoping to land an uppercut with her bony nose.

When he tightened her cinch after lunch each day she looked back at him with an expression of malignancy that could scarcely be misunderstood, uttering deep rumblings of protest from her grass-filled belly. And when he placed his foot in the stirrup she laid back her ears and tried to bite it. Certainly nothing could be clearer than that.

Just as all men think that their secretaries are in love with them, however, Mr. Robbins could never bring himself to believe that Dolly's overdeveloped heart did not beat faster with pleasure when she saw him approaching and he felt tenderly toward her because of it as he met her at the hitching rail each morning.

This feeling of affection was apt to be pretty well dissipated, however, after the first hour on the trail, for

no matter what horse Dolly followed, she invariably fell behind. Her legs seemed shackled by an invisible hobble which prevented her from putting one foot as far in front of the other as ordinary horses. To make up for this it would have been logical for her to have quickened her pace, but whatever rudimentary logic Dolly possessed seemed to be in reverse. As she fell further behind, her head would droop in sleep until only the exasperated drumming of Mr. Robbins' heels on her impervious ribs would cause her to close up the gap at a sullen trot, thus forcing the annoyed riders immediately behind her to do likewise and those at the end of the column to canter.

Dolly's difficulties in keeping up with her contemporaries were great enough on level ground, but on steep downhill grades and when crossing streams they smacked of the neurotic. Basically she was a mass of psychic fears. Being tipped downward caused her to tremble violently and she conceived of evil spirits lurking beneath all running waters. In view of the fact

that she was going down a slope or crossing a stream every few minutes, her mind was necessarily in a constant state of agitation.

When the descending trail became particularly steep and rocky Dolly merely minced up and down with her front feet, blew her nose violently and emitted deep groans, all of which gave the impression of activity but produced no forward motion.

Confronted with a stream she planted both feet on the bank and stared at its moving surface with bulging eyes. Finally, impelled into action by Mr. Robbins' boot heels, she placed her nose in the water and inched across, accompanying her progress with violent internal rumblings stating as plainly as words that such folly could only end in disaster.

On reaching the opposite bank her relief was so great that she expressed it by bounding from the stream like

an antelope and continuing down the trail in a series of joyous leaps until she caught up with her companions. This caused Mr. Robbins much physical and mental anguish until he found that, by clinging to the saddle horn with both hands, he became glued to the saddle, a discovery that gained him a considerable reputation for horsemanship from those who witnessed these episodes from the rear.

For the most part, Dolly had no recourse against this mad rib-thumper who insisted upon eating his lunches in the most inaccessible spots in the Rocky Mountains. On the heavily wooded trails, however, she was given occasional opportunities for retaliation which she seldom missed. Knowing to an inch how far the knees of her tormentor stuck out, she devoted her entire attention to cracking them against the trees on either side of the trail.

It was a grim game in which Mr. Robbins frequently found himself clutching a pine tree with both hands in an effort to either push the tree away from Dolly or Dolly away from the tree. Occasionally this would end in a scraping noise and a deep groan, causing Dolly's ears to turn back and a soft look of pleasure to come into her brown eyes.

The relationship between a male and a female, however, is as devious as it is unpredictable. When Old Hank said to Mr. Robbins one morning at the corral, "Now that Mr. Brandon's gone you might as well have his hoss if you want. Might be better ridin' than that old nag Dolly," Mr. Robbins found himself saying, "No, thanks. Dolly and I have been through too much grief together. She's almost knocked me to pieces and she ought to have a chance to finish the job. Besides which Dolly's no nag. She's the best trail horse you've got."

At the sound of Mr. Robbins' voice Dolly, asleep at the hitching rail, opened her eyes and turned her head slowly in his direction. Then, apparently not liking what she saw, she shut them again and went back to sleep.

Mrs. Weller panted up the rise to the Robbinses' cabin. "I'll never get used to this altitude," she said, sinking into a canvas chair on the porch.

The rays of the sun were warm, but a cool breeze blew down from Sawtooth giving notice that the backbone of summer, if not broken, was at least cracking. Wood smoke drifted from the two chimneys of the cabin.

"I've never been so comfortable or so contented in all my life," said Mrs. Robbins, moving her chair further into the sunlight. "It's just too good to be true. I know something's going to break the spell."

"I am," said Mrs. Weller. "I've just been talking to Mary and Tom about the pack trip."

"What pack trip?" asked Mrs. Robbins in alarm.

"Not me," said Mr. Robbins. "I'm not going to leave my nice comfortable bed and sleep on a lot of cold rocks for anybody."

"And wake up all frowzy and brush our teeth in front of a lot of strangers. Oh, Jane. I just couldn't."

Mr. Weller had wandered over from his half of the cabin in time to hear this last remark. "Don't brush them," he said. "Just let the wind blow through them. It's much less conspicuous."

Mrs. Weller waved this banter aside with an impatient gesture. "But Sally, you know that this was all agreed on back in New York. And Mary told me this morning that there is such a demand for pack trips that she had only one open date. She's going to send us into the game country for three days, starting Monday. It seemed to me I'd better clinch the opportunity before someone else grabbed it so I said we'd go. And Mr. Perkins and Mr. Hosker and Mrs. Taylor are coming."

"Of course three days might not be so bad," said Mr. Robbins thoughtfully. "It's long trips that I don't like."

"But it's impossible, darling. How in the world could we leave Bobby for three days?" asked Mrs. Robbins.

"He'll be all right," said Mr. Weller. "I'll bet you haven't seen him in the last three days, anyhow."

"He's going with us," said Mr. Robbins unexpectedly. There was a strained silence, broken by Mrs. Robbins.

"Oh, Horace, do you think—?"

"It's absurd," said Mrs. Weller. "Children don't go on this kind of a trip."

"This one does," said Mr. Robbins, "or else."

"Well, of course, if you feel like that about it," said Mrs. Weller.

"We're off," cried Mr. Weller, the peacemaker. "Off on the trail of the lonesome pine."

"Well, I'm so relieved you all want to go," said Mrs. Weller. "I was afraid you might not want to. I'll just go down right now and confirm it with Mary."

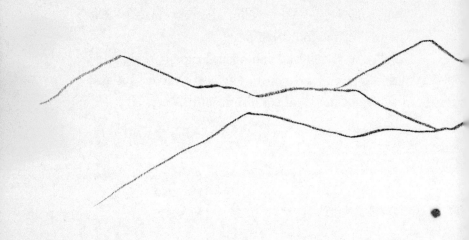

own at the Bar Z Bar corral seven mules stood at the hitching rail with bowed, dejected heads. Only yesterday they had been carefree, happy mules, grazing in a mountain pasture. Now they were about to be loaded with battered carrying boxes and huge bales containing the endless paraphernalia so essential to pack-trippers desiring to live the primitive life in the manner to which they have been accustomed.

The trip which loomed over their unhappy backs on this particular morning was only going to be out for two nights and three days, but to a casual observer the preparations at the corral might easily have been in anticipation of an expedition to Outer Mongolia.

From the ranch houses people were moving in small groups to watch the packing and ultimately to wave godspeed to the adventurers. Pack trips were going out constantly, but despite that fact they always created an atmosphere of special excitement in the life of the ranch. Perhaps they stirred dim, atavistic memories, faint recallings of long-past days when men set forth into the wilderness on missions from which, occasionally, they did not return.

The mission of this particular pack trip was somewhat vague. It was going out to look for game, not for purposes of subsistence—that was carried on the backs of the mules—but merely for the pleasure of the search.

The searchers were a motley group; the Robbinses and the Wellers, the talkative Mr. Perkins, whose wife would have nothing to do with pack trips, the alluring Mrs. Taylor, Mr. Hosker, a newcomer who in a brief period had established a reputation for encyclopedic learning, as well as (to the great disgust of the Wellers) Bobby.

These were the adventurers who eventually moved out from the corral, headed by Old Hank, with Slim and the Reimses' attractive daughter, Polly, riding herd at the end of the column. Old Hank towed the lead mules by his halter rope, the others were hitched together ignominiously head to tail in a long line. All seven were half buried under huge packs which swayed from side to side as they walked, giving the procession the appearance of an oriental caravan.

Hour after hour they plodded along the wooded edge of a narrow valley. Ahead of them a new range of mountains emerged slowly from the blue-gray haze. Its central peak blocked the valley with its great head-wall—bare, inaccessible, inhospitable, its ancient brown wrinkles still packed with last winter's snow.

"Simba," said Mr. Hosker. "Discovered by A. K. Parker in 1845."

"Mercy," said Mrs. Robbins, who was riding in front of him and felt that some acknowledgment of this helpful information was called for.

Late in the afternoon they reached a grove of trees on the edge of the meadows through which a brook rushed youthfully down from the forested hillside to throw in its lot with the stream which wound through the middle of the valley. There were evidences of an old campfire beneath the trees.

"This is it," said Old Hank, "might as well go fishin' as soon as I break out your rods. Ain't nothin' to do on a pack trip but ride an' eat an' fish. You've done your ridin' an' you won't be eatin' for an hour or two. Bobby can stay here an' help set things up."

They spread out, up and down the stream. Mrs. Taylor had unearthed from the baggage pile a pair of brown hip boots, a brown suède fishing jacket with voluminous pockets and a jaunty little cap from under which escaped curly wisps of honey-colored hair. She attached herself to Mr. Robbins.

"I'm going with *you*," she said. "I need lots of advice and if you fish as well as you square dance you're my man."

"I really don't know much about it," said Mr. Robbins modestly. He had been debating whether to go fishing or lie under a tree and take a much-needed nap. He decided to go fishing.

"Well, I know exactly nothing at all," said Mrs. Taylor as they set off across the meadow. "So our combined I.Q. shouldn't worry the fish too much. That's all right with me because I really hope I *don't* catch anything. I wouldn't touch one of the slimy things on a bet. If something *should* get fastened onto my line you'll have to take it off. Else they can cook it on the hook."

If there was anything Mr. Robbins himself hated it was slobbering around with fish, but, judging by his own previous experience, the chances of Mrs. Taylor catching any were slim.

"Don't worry," he said, "I'll handle anything you bring ashore."

"You're a duck," she said, touching his arm lightly. "I'll fish in this cute little deep place and you go round the bend where you can be near me without catching your hook in my hairdo every time you wave it around."

The section of stream which Mrs. Taylor had assigned to Mr. Robbins was a broad, shallow stretch in which no self-respecting trout would have been found dead. Before he had disentangled his line, which was snarled as usual, he heard her give an excited scream.

She was standing in the middle of the stream, her rod bent nearly double. "I think it's a sturgeon or a codfish or something," she called. "I've been trying to shake him loose, but he won't get off. Hurry up and give me a hand before I throw the rod at him and go home."

She had landed her fish by the time he reached her. The trout lay flopping in the grass, a fine fourteen-incher. Overcoming his repulsion, Mr. Robbins seized it by the middle, only to have it shoot out of his grasp like a watermelon seed. "You ought to wear abrasive gloves," said Mrs. Taylor.

The fish had swallowed the hook like a sleeping

pill. Ten minutes later, Mr. Robbins washed his hands distastefully in the cold water.

"There's a place in this jacket for carrying fish," said Mrs. Taylor, "but nuts with that. If you knew what it cost you'd agree. It's the last fish I ever expect to catch and I'm not going to smell like a fish market the rest of my life just for one trout. You take it like an old bunny and put it in *your* pocket."

Mr. Robbins carried the still-wriggling trout back to the place where he had been fishing and put it in his landing net. Before he could find his rod, which he had mislaid somewhere in the grass, Mrs. Taylor screamed again. "I'm being eaten alive by trout," she called. "Do come back."

The second unhooking was an equally nerve-racking operation which left Mr. Robbins almost as exhausted as the trout. "I'll just stay here," he said. "You won't lose so much time."

"I'm through with this place," said Mrs. Taylor. "I don't want to force my luck. Let's work downstream." She seemed to have suddenly forgotten her desire not to catch fish.

He followed her. At the unlikely shallow spot where he had been about to fish she caught her third. The sun was setting when they eventually started back. Mr. Robbins' landing net was so heavy with Mrs. Taylor's fish that he had to carry it over his shoulder, where its clammy contents slapped against his back at each weary step.

"You're a honey bunch," she said, as the smoke from their campfire and the tinkling bells of the hobbled horses welcomed them across the meadow.

The cook tent was up, a big white canvas affair of the type favored as a background by Civil War gen-

erals when being photographed by Brady. Behind it was an incongruous row of gaily striped square tents looking for all the world like the background of a medieval battle scene.

"How perfect," said Mrs. Taylor. "The field of Agincourt with General Grant in command. All we need are a few suits of armor hanging over the line to dry."

They sat before Old Hank's fire on the trunk of a

fallen tree, drinking whisky and ice-cold brook water out of tin cups, and watching Polly working around the cook fire with the sure, competent movements of an old hand.

To the west, two low hills jutted into the valley overlapping where it curved to the south. Behind them the cloudless sky turned to a cold greenish yellow. The two hills gradually became black silhouettes against the afterglow until they finally lost all semblance of reality and turned into a stage set at the Metropolitan Opera.

"Look," said Mr. Robbins. "There's the good old dipper."

"And Sirius," said Mr. Hosker. "Sirius is in ascendancy tonight. And did you ever see the Lesser Pleiades more clearly?"

Mr. Robbins, who did not have the slightest idea what Mr. Hosker was talking about, nodded assent. "Sure are," he said, contentedly.

The air grew colder as darkness came on. By the light of the fire they ate soup and steaks and corn on the cob, and drank huge cups of black coffee without a thought as to what it might do to their night's sleep.

The moon came up. Slim had thrown some logs on the cook fire, but the circle about them was forced to move steadily closer to absorb their warmth.

"I'm going to turn in," said Mr. Weller, "before I roast on one side and deep freeze on the other. You and I are tent mates, Robbins. I hope you laid your bedroll out before dark."

Mr. Robbins had not given his sleeping arrangements a thought up to that moment. "I guess I'd better look things over," he said, with a nonchalance he did not feel. He had no desire to sleep, but a man couldn't sit out all night and freeze to death just because he didn't want to come to grips with a sleeping bag.

"I'm going to sleep outside," said Mrs. Weller. "Down by the ladies' quarters. Admission by appointment only."

"Me, too," said Mr. Perkins. "Not on the harem side, of course. Hosker and I have bedded ourselves down behind the cook tent where we can count the stars before we go to sleep."

"He doesn't need to count them," said Mrs. Taylor. "He's known how many there are since he was a baby."

"I've put my roll outside right near your tent, Gramp," said Bobby.

"Bobby, I'm *not* going to have you sleeping out on that cold ground all night," said Mrs. Robbins.

"The ground *inside* ain't steam heated," said Old Hank.

Mrs. Robbins sighed and dropped the subject.

"I think you're all quite mad," said Mrs. Taylor. "Polly's cooking me some filler for my hot-water bottle. Then I'm going to wrap myself around it, roll down to the bottom of my bag and hibernate."

Mr. Weller had a large electric torch which revealed the fact that their tent, which had looked so gay and medieval in the sunset, was in reality a miserable box less than five feet high and about six feet square at the bottom. He had laid out his sleeping bag neatly on one side. His gear was placed in an orderly row along its edge. Now he closed the tent flap and tied it securely with a series of tapes. "There," he said to Mr. Robbins. "Snug as a bug in a rug."

To Mr. Robbins "rug" wasn't quite the word. He began to feel as Tutankhamen might have felt had he been able to watch his Egyptian undertakers putting the final seals on his tomb.

Mr. Weller sat on his bedroll and undressed methodically. He then put on a pair of Canton flannel pajamas, complete with feet, and slid into his bag like a seal. "Good night, old man," he said. "Pleasant dreams and sweet repose." Throwing the flap of the sleeping bag over his head he began almost immediately to snore.

"Same to you," muttered Mr. Robbins absently. Crouching in the restricted rays of Mr. Weller's flashlight he examined his side of the tent with dismay. His sleeping bag was a shapeless, twisted heap, disclosing neither beginning nor end. Around it, under it and on top of it, in a hopeless jumble, were his clothing and equipment which some big-heart had flung into the tent when the mules were unpacked.

Mr. Robbins had little experience with sleeping bags and this one looked particularly complicated. As he looked over its ramified flaps and straps it reminded him of a strait jacket. What an ugly thought!

He laid the bag out as best he could, rolled it on what appeared to be its back and eventually found the open-

ing into which he was apparently supposed to inject his body. To his consternation he discovered that the interior of the bag was filled with blankets, fixed in some kind of a circular arrangement like the chocolate layer rolls which his wife was always putting on for her more fancy dinners.

Having located what he took to be the core of the thing, he stuck a wet sneaker into the place as a marker and prepared for the night.

It was deathly cold in the tent. Once again the idea of a tomb crossed his mind as he glanced at the row of neatly tied tapes with which Mr. Weller had fastened the tent flap.

Hastily stripping to his long underwear, he pulled on a pair of white woolen socks, drew an old black football sweater over his head and inserted his feet in the indicated spot in the bedroll.

Judging by the ease with which Mr. Weller had slid into his, Mr. Robbins concluded that either he or it must have been greased. Every time Mr. Robbins tried to wriggle down into the roll, the blankets wriggled down with him. Finally, by holding them tightly with both hands, he managed to reach the bottom, but only after causing serious internal derangements.

He turned out the flashlight and lay quite still in the chaos of bedding. Several things became immediately evident. One, the air mattress beneath the sleeping bag had been displaced in the struggle so that the bag and the mattress formed a kind of letter X. Two, as a result his head was resting on the ground several inches below his shoulders. Three, there was some sort of a steel spine just under his own.

He tried, by a series of convulsive motions, to bring the sleeping bag into line with the mattress, but only ended by hitching the whole thing forward so that the bottom of the bag rested on a pile of unidentified duffel in the corner of the tent. His head was nested in a hollow in the ground. Releasing one hand, he clawed the scattered equipment beside him into a pile that he hoped might turn out to be a pillow, only to find his head now resting on his camera and his tin fly box. He turned his attention to the metallic ridge beneath him.

It was the zipper of the sleeping bag. Shouldn't that be on the side of the bag? With a violent effort he managed to turn his body to one side, hoping to turn the bag at the same time. In doing so he wrapped the inner blankets around him like twisted taffy. Trapped, immobilized, he lay quite still, like an animal run to earth. He had been in bed (if that was what you called it) for ten minutes. He freed his left hand so that he could see the luminous dial of his wrist watch. It was ten-fifteen. Even if he got up at five-thirty he would have to lie here, imprisoned, unable to move, for almost seven hours.

Inch by inch he managed to turn onto the other side, thus untwisting the blankets slightly, but reducing their inner arrangement to incomprehensible confusion. Exhausted, he dozed fitfully for a while, then came starkly, irretrievably awake. Surely the dawn couldn't be far away. The hands of his watch pointed to ten minutes after eleven. The contents of the sleeping bag had once more twined themselves around him like a python. On the other side of the tiny tent pole Weller was making a noise like a sawmill. He became conscious of squirming, writhing nerves filling his body like the closely packed wires in a telephone cable.

HE HAD TO GET OUT OF HERE! Panic swept over him suddenly, like a wave. HE HAD TO GET OUT OF HERE!

Mr. Robbins had always ridiculed people who complained of claustrophobia. Now he felt it descending on him like a suffocating cloud. Hysterically, he wriggled out of the bedroll, turning it more or less inside out in the process. It was bitter cold. He reached for the light and came in contact with Mr. Weller's face. The latter gave a loud snort and awoke.

"Wha'sa matter?" he mumbled.

"I can't find the light," said Mr. Robbins.

Mr. Weller sat up, found the light and flashed it

on Mr. Robbins' bed. "Good God," he said, "what's been going on? You been having a wrestling match with a grizzly or something?"

"I can't sleep," said Mr. Robbins.

"So I see," said Mr. Weller. "I told you you ought to straighten out your bedroll before dark. The trouble with you is—"

"I've got to get out of here." Mr. Robbins struggled to keep hysteria out of his voice.

"Where you going?" asked Mr. Weller sleepily.

"Anywhere," said Mr. Robbins. "I'm going to walk in the woods. ANYWHERE."

Mr. Weller turned the light on Mr. Robbins and his face registered alarm. Leaning forward he began to unlace the fastenings of the tent flap with some haste. "O.K.," he said, drawing it aside. "Excuse me, old man, if I don't come with you."

Mr. Robbins crawled through the opening into the night. The moon flooded the meadow and the grove with an uncanny, silvery radiance. From somewhere off to the left he could hear the sound of the bells where the horses and mules were grazing. He took several deep breaths of the icy air. Its chill reminded him that he had nothing on but a pair of long white woolen underdrawers and a black sweater. Behind the tents an abandoned logging road led from the grove into the thick woods that rose above it. To keep warm, or, to be more accurate, to keep from freezing, Mr. Robbins walked cautiously up its rough, moonlit surface.

Behind the cook tent Mr. Hosker and Mr. Perkins lay in their sleeping bags gazing, wide-eyed, at the sky. They lay quite still, neither one wishing the other to know that he was unable to sleep. The bigness of their surroundings was making them a bit jumpy.

At the same instant they both saw a pair of white legs move silently into a patch of moonlight. They were unquestionably human legs, but the terrifying thing about them was that they were unaccompanied by a body.

While they watched in silent and lonely horror the trunkless legs disappeared into the woods. Each concluded that when one drank whisky out of big tin cups

there was a tendency to pour too freely. Each shuddered, closed his eyes and pulled his head under the flap of his bedroll, resolved never to speak of the incident to a living soul.

The old logging road ended, a short distance up the side of the hill, in a tangle of fallen tree trunks. Mr. Robbins sat down on one of them. Then, as the cold began to bite into his bones, he realized that he must either return to the sleeping bag or freeze to death. Of the two, the sleeping bag seemed preferable, now that he was out of it, and he retraced his steps down the hill.

To his surprise Bobby met him at the edge of the wood. "I heard you, Gramp. I heard you talking to Mr. Weller. Then I saw you go up into the woods. It's nice out where I'm sleeping so I dragged your sleeping bag out of that old tent and put it by mine. Is that O.K.?"

"It sure is," said Mr. Robbins gratefully.

His bedroll was laid out neatly beside Bobby's, its flap opened at the right place. "Good night, Gramp," said Bobby, sliding into his. "It's been fun doing things together this summer, hasn't it?"

"It sure has," said Mr. Robbins, surprised and suddenly sleepy.

The sound of voices woke him. The bedroll, which had seemed so hostile a few hours before, was now a warm, protective nest. Raising his head slightly he could see Polly hovering over the cooking fire. A few yards further down the slope Slim was squatting on his heels beside the little brook.

With an effort of will, Mr. Robbins wriggled out of the warm blankets into the clear, winelike air, already beginning to warm in the early-morning sunlight. Having found a towel and a cake of soap he walked down to the brook and tried to squat beside it like Slim.

To his chagrin he found that his knees wouldn't bend much beyond a right angle. Feeling that Polly and Slim were probably watching, he pretended to be looking for something in the grass. Then he tried straddling the brook, but it had worn such a deep groove into the surface of the meadow that he could not bend down far enough to reach the water. He sat down on the edge and placed his feet on the opposite bank, but again he could not reach the brook. This was becoming silly. Cleanliness might be next to godliness but in the West it was next to impossible for a man who couldn't squat.

Lying full length on the dew-soaked grass he finally managed to splash water on his face and hair. He returned, dripping, to the fire, the front of his blue jeans and shirt drenched with dew. Mr. and Mrs. Weller were seated on the fallen tree drinking coffee. They looked at Mr. Robbins with surprise.

"What in the world happened to you, old man?" asked Mr. Weller. "First you go screaming into the night in your underclothes and then, when I wake up this morning, your bed's gone, too. Don't you ever just relax and spend the night sleeping?"

"And then, apparently, he goes in swimming at dawn with his clothes on," said Mrs. Weller, observing Mr. Robbins' soaked shirt and trousers.

"If he does he must skim around on his stomach like a water bug," said Mr. Weller, "because he's all dry in back."

"Breakfast is ready," said Polly.

"Come and get it," yelled Mr. Weller leaping from the log and seizing a tin plate from the top of a pile that was warming beside the fire.

They were off for the day in search of game. Polly and six lucky mules had been left behind to tend camp.

"If you want to see any game," warned Old Hank, as they crossed the valley and started up the opposite slope, "you got to cut out the yackety-yack."

Thus admonished they climbed in silence through the lodgepoles and the Douglas firs. Enforced quiet was a particular hardship for Mr. Perkins and Mrs. Taylor, to whom talking was as essential as breathing. They were riding at the rear of the column, just ahead of Slim.

Mrs. Taylor could stand it no longer. "Do you know the Britehearts in Philadelphia?" she asked, half turning in her saddle and addressing Mr. Perkins.

"You mean Ann and George Briteheart? I should say I do."

"Now isn't that something," cried Mrs. Taylor. "Ann Briteheart was one of my bridesmaids. She was Ann Trexel. Then she married Sam Abercrombie."

"That didn't turn out too well, did it?" asked Mr. Perkins. They were emerging from the woods onto a large upland meadow. Old Hank scanned its borders with a pair of ancient binoculars.

"I'll say it didn't," said Mrs. Taylor. "Poor Ann gave him two children. Then he gave them back to her and was never heard from again."

"I think," said Old Hank, "that if we follow that ridge up to where you see that big open place on the shoulder you might see something."

"Do we have to keep quiet *now?*" asked Mr. Perkins.

"Well, 'twouldn't do no harm to start practicing," said Old Hank.

They climbed where only broad-chested, mountain-bred horses could; through forest glades carpeted with multicolored flowers, coming into bloom a month later than their lowland cousins, past dust-grimed pockets of snow from whose lower edges small streams departed on their long journey back to the sea, scrambling over outcroppings of rock above the timber line, with the mountains unfolding their purple ruggedness to the horizon and then, finally, standing at the top of the snow-pocketed pass with the world spread out before them on either side.

"As I remember it," said Mrs. Taylor, "Sara Henderson married one of the two brothers."

"Jack," said Mr. Perkins. "They broke up in Paris."

Looking down it seemed impossible that anything short of a mountain goat could negotiate the faint trail that hairpinned back and forth across the mountain-

side beneath them. Old Hank headed down, however, without a moment's hesitation and the others followed only because there was no other place to go.

"I think I'll close my eyes," said Mrs. Taylor.

"I can't. My horse is asleep," said Mr. Perkins. "Somebody's got to stay awake to drive."

In spite of the apparent odds against it, they reached the bottom quite safely and headed across a broad valley toward another range. Old Hank pulled up sharply and pointed. "Look," he said.

Coming up over the brow of a bare mountain, half a mile ahead, were six bull elk. They saw the riders and stopped to inspect them. Mr. Perkins said, "I met my sister-in-law in Rome and we took a plane that night. . . . What's the trouble up there?"

They stood motionless watching the elk and the latter stood equally frozen watching the riders. Then the leader, sensing danger, wheeled and took off along the ridge until he reached some unseen trail leading down the other side. In a moment they were lost to view.

Mrs. Taylor said, "I adore Rome. We spent the winter there two years ago. Jack was a great friend of Mrs. Luce. . . ."

They climbed to the spot where the elk had stood and found to their surprise that they were on a shoulder of Simba, the mountain beneath which they had slept the previous night. A cold wind was howling across the narrow ridge, causing the horses to turn their backs to it with clamped-down tails as the party paused to take in the view. Far, far below were the lodgepole forests and the meadow and the meandering hairline of the stream.

Miles ahead, a wisp of smoke rose above the trees. A thousand feet directly beneath them, the headwall of Simba fell off sheer and impassable. If the mountain had looked forbidding from the valley floor it looked even more so now, only here it was the bottomland which had become inaccessible. Old Hank pointed to the thin column of smoke and grinned. "Supper's cookin'," he said.

A rain squall was approaching up the valley. "Looks like we might get a bit damp," said Old Hank. "If anybody wants to dismount and put on their slicker this is about the last chance they'll get for quite a while."

"That rain won't hit *us*," said Mr. Weller. "It's going across the valley." He remained mounted while the others got off, unfastened their slickers from their saddles and put them on.

"Let's go," said Old Hank, and started along the ridge on the path the elk had taken. Mr. Weller rode in front of Mr. Robbins.

The ridge grew narrower until they felt as if they were walking a tightrope among the clouds, and then the storm broke, the icy rain whipping against them mercilessly. Mr. Weller reached behind him and started to untie the thongs holding his raincoat.

Slim, riding at the rear of the column, saw him. "Don't put that slicker on while you're on your horse," he yelled above the wind. "And you can't dismount here."

"What does that half-baked cowpuncher think I'm going to do? Catch pneumonia? To heck with him," said Mr. Weller, continuing to struggle with the wet knots.

Slim left his position at the end of the line and came squeezing past the riders, his horse barely finding footing on the razor-backed ridge. His usually good-natured face was set and hard.

"Don't take that slicker off your saddle," he said to Mr. Weller.

"Listen," said Mr. Weller, "you can't tell me . . ."

"I'm telling you," said Slim. He stopped his horse and let the others crowd past him until he was again at the rear of the column. Mr. Weller abandoned his attempt to untie the slicker.

"Weller," said Mr. Robbins to the former's rain-soaked back, "you're an ass."

He was surprised by his own words and by the vehemence with which they were uttered. And then a great feeling of peace stole over him which counteracted the rain and the biting wind and made him feel warm and contented to the core of his being.

"That's telling 'em, Gramp," said a small voice behind him.

Mr. and Mrs. Robbins, with Bobby sleeping on the back seat, drove eastward over the great lonely plains of northeastern Wyoming. The Wellers had gone to visit their daughter and son-in-law in Denver.

The atmosphere was relaxed, but there was a sadness to this home trek, for the West had cast its spell on them all. Its mountains and streams and dark green forests were pulling them back like powerful magnets. They drove in silence while across the screen of their minds passed glimpses of wooded, flower-bordered trails, of mountain lakes, reflecting the rocky faces of overhanging cliffs, of blue smoke rising from campfires, twisting brooks burrowing through the valley grass, sage, jagged, snow-flecked peaks, the glitter of frosty stars—a never-ending reel of color and beauty.

They could smell the trail dust, the pungent odor of sweat-soaked leather and the scent of the forest after a rain. They could hear the click of a hoof on a fallen tree, the soft, ripping sound of grass torn by a horse's teeth, the continuous rumble of a mountain thunderstorm and the whistle of a trout line.

Each sensed what was going through the mind of the other. "It wasn't only the place, though," said Mr. Robbins, breaking the silence. "It was the people. You got so doggone fond of the people."

"I know," said Mrs. Robbins. "If you went back after everybody had gone I suppose it wouldn't be the same place at all. And the funny part of it is that you fall in love with all those people and you miss them so when they leave the ranch that you want to go home yourself, yet a lot of them live around New York and I'll bet we won't see much of them this winter. The minute we get back we'll all pick up our old lives where we left them off, and the spell is broken."

Mr. Robbins pondered this idea for several miles. "Perhaps the charm of a ranch lies in the fact that people change when they come to it. Not permanently. I don't mean that. Just while they're there. I think it's because for once in their lives they stop competing. They wear the same crazy clothes, they do the same things together every day and everybody knows what everybody else is doing. That's the point. There's nothing to compete about. It's the nearest thing I know to what tribal life must have been—even if it *is* on a de luxe scale. Perhaps modern man misses his old tribal life more than he knows."

Mrs. Robbins nodded absently. She sidestepped these metaphysical discussions. "It certainly did wonders for Bobby," she said. "He's a different child."

There was a stirring on the back seat. Bobby sat up rubbing his eyes. "When do we eat?" he asked sleepily.

Streeter, Edward
   Mr. Robbins rides again.

RULES

1. Books marked 7 days may be kept one week.
Books marked 14 days, two weeks. The latter
may be renewed if more than 6 months old.

2. A fine of two cents a day will be charged
on each book which is not returned according to
the above rule. No book will be issued to any
person having a fine of 25 cents or over.

3. A charge of ten cents will be made for
mutilated plastic jackets. All injuries to books
beyond reasonable wear and all losses shall be
made good to the satisfaction of the Librarian.

4. Each borrower is held responsible for all
books drawn on his card and for all fines accru-
ing on the same.